LANDS FAR AWAY

Stephen Brooke

Eggshell Boats 2021

Lands Far Away ©2021 Stephen Brooke

ISBN 978-1-937745-79-0

Arachis Press
4803 Peanut Road
Graceville, FL 32440
http://arachispress.com

Please note that this is not a book for children. Though there is nothing graphic in these fantastic tales, there is material in them that may not be suited to younger readers.

CONTENTS

Beyond

Stories

"ALL THE BEST stories happened once upon a time in lands far away," claimed Luis.

His sister was inclined to be skeptical. "When was once upon a time?"

"Long ago. Before you were born." He gave the question a further moment of thought. "Before Grandpa was born!"

"That would be a long time," Rebecca agreed, her eyes flicking for just a moment to that grandfather, ensconced in a nearby, well-cushioned chair. He couldn't decide whether or not she was being sarcastic.

"Once upon a time was just as long ago when I was your age as it is now," he told them.

Luis frowned. "Is that possible?"

"It is in lands far away. Those are always just as far away no matter how long you travel." His eyes seemed to search for those lands, for just a few seconds. "Always over the next hill or around the corner or even across the sea."

"So how do we get there?" asked the girl.

"Your brother already told us. They're in all the best stories."

"I'd like to go there," declared Luis, a bit dreamily. "To lands far away."

"Then Grandpa should take us," said Rebecca. "He knows all the best stories."

"Only some of them," the old man informed her. "No one can know all that happened in far away lands, once upon a time. We keep finding new stories, no matter how many we already know. Settle down here by me and I'll go looking for one. Ah, yes, that should do."

And so he began.

Boy

THERE WAS A boy named Boy. If his family had owned a dog, perhaps they would have called it 'Boy' but as they didn't, his father decided to use it for his son. "What is he if he isn't a boy?" he reasoned. His wife had no ready answer but still didn't much like it.

His brothers and sisters—and they were numerous—had more normal names. There were Ted and Tom and Alice. Jœ and Maria and Patty and Linda too. Is that all? One, two—yes, seven of them. Boy made eight.

Now, you may have heard of a boy named Boy before. There was one in the Tarzan movies, but not in the books. He was given the perfectly good name of Jack there. Hmm, I am getting away from our story, aren't I?

All of this was once upon a time, of course, and, yes, in far away lands. Boy set out to make his fortune in those far away lands, one morning. He was tall now, taller than his father, and yearned to cross the hills and the seas. But he had gotten no further than the dirt road winding through the middle of his village when Rosa called to him from an upstairs window.

"Are you a good boy?" she asked, and laughed.

Rosa had dark hair and eyes and a merry smile and Boy rather liked her. "I'm going to fetch," he told her and continued on his way. Maybe he would come back someday and see her again.

Maybe he would not. As he strolled down the sunlit way, Boy pulled forth a small flute he had made of a reed. He might not have gotten the fingering holes in quite the right places so it was a little out of tune, but he didn't care. He played past the mill on the edge of the village, and on into the open country beyond.

By noon, he was in lands he didn't know. Boy had a vague idea that other villages existed, down the road. After all, a road must lead somewhere, right? But for all he knew, if he followed it till evening he might come back to his own village from the other end.

He had no idea of the size of the world. That had never been a problem before. Ahead, he saw a wagon beside the pathway. It was unlike any wagon he had ever seen before, more like a box, and he saw no way one might fill it with hay or turnips. Boy was curious and became more curious as he drew closer. That usually worked out the other way around.

He could see bars on the side of the wagon and a reclining form inside. A corpulent man sat beside it on a three-legged stool, eating his lunch. His gown had surely been black once but had faded to a rusty tone. Boy nodded a hello and peered into the wagon-cage.

"What is it?" he asked. It seemed to have wings.

"Why, that's a griffin, lad."

Boy gave it another look. It was about the size of one of the miller's mastiffs, but looked less fearsome. It gazed back at him with yellow cat eyes. "I thought they were bigger."

The man chuckled. "Think on it, boy. His father was an eagle and his mother a lion. You can't expect him to grow larger than his parents, can you?"

Boy was larger than his parents but felt that wasn't pertinent. "Haven't I heard of folks, um, riding on them?

"Not on griffins. One needs a hippogriff for that and that's exactly why I cart this chimera about the countryside. He's at stud. There are those who will pay well for his services." He seemed pleased by that thought and not so pleased by the one that followed. "In between, I can make a few pennies displaying him in villages."

He looked the lanky lad over. "I'm Guy D'Laniger. Sit down and have a bite, why don't you?" Boy took a place beside him, on the ground. The man handed over a chunk of stale bread and moldy cheese. "That's about it for my hospitality, boy, until I have some more of those pennies. You don't mind if I call you Boy, do you?"

"Everyone else does."

Guy passed him a crock. Boy cautiously sniffed—it had a pungent unfamiliar odor about it—and took a sip. Only a sip. He politely did not spit it out. "What is it, sir?"

The man cocked his head at him. "Naught but an ordinary red wine. You've had wine before, haven't you, Boy?"

"Only my grandmother's elderberry wine. It is not, uh, much like this."

"I can imagine. Now say, Boy, might you be interested in a job? My last keeper—er, assistant—left me kind of sudden-like and I could use a lad like you. At least as long as we're traveling the same way." He regarded the young man for a moment, before deciding, "I'll pay you a penny a week."

Boy stared at him in amazement, unable to answer. That seemed like untold riches to him.

"Oh, okay, make it tuppence," said Guy D'Laniger, misinterpreting. "No more!"

"Yes, sir!" said his new assistant, finding his tongue.

Guy got the one old piebald nag pulling the wagon to start moving at a leisurely pace. Both walked alongside, kicking up the red dust of the road. After a while, Boy pulled out his flute and began another tuneless tune.

What was that sound? He hadn't noticed it at first. Was someone humming along?

"Penrithega likes your playing," Guy observed. "He's purring. Never known him to take to anyone like that before." He seemed to hesitate a few seconds before admitting, "My previous assistant didn't exactly quit out of the blue. Old Pen bit his hand off one day. He can be dangerous, lad. Reckon you should know that."

That cruel curved beak did look dangerous. Whether the talons up front or the paws with claws at back might do more damage, Boy couldn't decide. Either might well kill one who got too close. "What does Penrithega eat?" he asked.

"Meat and nothing but meat. He's expensive to maintain." Guy attempted a weak grin that looked more like a grimace. "Pen might have been a bit peckish when he went for Samkin. Would have eaten all of him, given the chance."

Boy decided to make certain Pen was always well fed. It was too bad the griffin couldn't be let out to hunt on his own but he much doubted he would return to his cage. He played another tune as they tramped along. It sounded much like the one before it.

The next day they reached a village and a couple days later another. There was more to this world than Boy had realized. "Good news, Boy," Guy told him after disappearing into a tavern for some time. "There's a local farmer with too much money and a mare ready to breed."

Boy gave him a blank look.

"He wants to make a hippogriff. That takes a griffin for a sire and a mare for the mother."

"What if one did the opposite?" wondered Boy. "A stallion and a female griffin?"

"There are no female griffins. That's why the beasts go after horses."

And why they were rare, decided Boy. At least, he'd never seen but one and he'd been to three villages now. "Have you heard, Penny?" he asked the winged creature as he fed him that evening. "You're going to have a ladyfriend tomorrow." As Penrithega tore apart a couple chickens—he swallowed his food whole, eagle-style—Boy played for him on his reed flute. The griffin always seemed to enjoy listening. He was less irritable too.

Not surprisingly, D'Laniger urged Boy to play often and long. A placid griffin was much to be preferred over the evil-tempered Penrithega he had come to know and fear. "Keep the music going," he said, as they trundled toward Farmer Hamm's stead the next morning. That Hamm was well-to-do was obvious. His fields were wide, his cattle many, his house large.

Not surprisingly, he was willing to bargain long to get the best price for Pen's services. When at last an amount was agreed upon, the farmer led them to his mare. Guy seemed just a little surprised to behold a rather large draft mare but, of course, the customer is always right. Whether a hippogriff of draft horse size could get off the ground was not his concern.

"I can not be responsible for any damage done to your mare," he once again warned Hamm. "Sometimes he'll just decide he's hungry rather than amorous."

"Oh, I have some insurance to make sure your griffin behaves. In fact, here she comes now." He turned to Guy and Boy and, for that matter, Penrithega, and announced, looking up, "That's Bertha."

A dragon was spiraling down toward them. Boy had no idea whether it was a large dragon as it was the first he had ever seen. It was gray. That he could tell. He might have expected a more outlandish color. Green, maybe.

Suddenly, Pen squalled loudly and took off, dragging D'Laniger behind him on the leash affixed to his collar. Guy went bumping along, hanging on, sometimes bouncing off the ground, sometimes a few feet above it.

The dragon settled into a landing beside Farmer Hamm. "Oh, I say, I didn't mean to spook it. Hamm asked me to drop by." She nodded toward the farmer, her sleek head bobbing atop its long neck. "He and I are old friends."

Said farmer was laughing uproariously. Boy noted that the horse was not in the least perturbed by the great beast's presence. She must be a frequent visitor.

"I do feel responsible. I'll try to catch up with them. Do you wish to come along, young man?"

"I don't think I could keep up," said Boy.

Bertha laughed too, though more decorously than Hamm. "I meant you could ride. Hop on!"

Why not? Boy took a seat behind her wings. The body was surprisingly thin, almost snake-like, but covered with coarse fur, not scales. He grabbed hold of that fur as Bertha the dragon launched herself into the clear morning air and sped in the direction they had last seen Penrithega and Guy D'Laniger. It was not long before they spied a black form on the ground below. The dragon alit near it.

D'Laniger had apparently fallen from some distance. "Oh dear. It seems your master is quite dead. He really should have let go of the leash sooner." She regarded the body thoughtfully for a moment or two. "I am rather surprised your griffin—"

"Penrithega," interjected Boy.

"Yes, quite. I am surprised Penrithega didn't stop to eat him. He must have had something else on his mind." Bertha rose into the air a short distance, looking all about as she hovered. "There."

Tracks. The imprints of the cloven hooves meant nothing to Boy.

"A unicorn. And in heat—I can tell from the scent," the dragon told him. "I wonder what sort of offspring could arise from that." Then she laughed. "Oh, but only a virgin can catch a unicorn. I am sure Penrithega does not qualify. Nor," she added, a little more seriously, "do I. Which is too bad, as I have been curious as to how they taste."

"Umm," began Boy.

Bertha raised an eyebrow. Or the dragon equivalent of one. "Oh. Well, let's get going then."

With Bertha's strong wings to carry them, they soon caught up with the griffin and the object of his affection. Somehow, Penrithega could just not connect with the unicorn, which eluded him no matter how ardently he attempted to corner the beautiful beast. She seemed to think it was a game. The sun shown on her very long and very sharp ivory horn as she tossed her head; she might be amused by the griffin at the moment but that weapon could be deadly if she changed her mind!

Boy slipped from the dragon's back and pulled forth his flute. At the first strands of his simple but haunting (and slightly out of tune) song, Penrithega began to settle down. Boy took a seat on the ground, playing on, and before long the griffin came to lie beside him, purring contentedly.

The unicorn looked long at the young man. Then she danced over to him, to lay her head in his lap. Boy stroked her neck and told her, "Get along now, girl." She bounded away, a flash of white disappearing into the woods.

"I suppose it wouldn't have been sporting to eat her," commented Bertha. She didn't sound completely sure of it.

The village was falling into dusk, the shadows of the houses lying long and purple across the street, when Boy arrived home, a week or so later. But Rosa was at her darkened window and spied him. "So what did you do while you were gone, Boy?" she called to him.

"I chased a cat!" he called back.

Penrithega padded silently at his side.

Beyond

a song

I'm bound beyond the fields we know——away!
Across the hills of man I go——away!
The horns of Færie call to me,
They tell of wonders I must see——away, far away!

My heart knows every tale fools tell——away!
The whispered seas within a shell——away!
A pœt gave me all his dreams,
A bag of riddles and moonbeams——away, far away!

The scattered leaves on wild winds borne——away!
Become my map, ancient and torn——away!
Beyond the edges of the world
My barque shall quest with sails unfurled——away, far away!

I'll seek where my horizons lie——away!
Where the sea becomes the sky——away!
To gaze upon the fabled lands
Where a mystic tower stands——away, far away!

An elfin princess slumbers there——away!
All robed in sheets of shining hair——away!
A kiss to rouse her from her sleep,
To lift her enchantment deep——away, far away!

I'm bound beyond the fields we know——away!
Across the hills of man I go——away!
The horns of Færie call to me,
They tell of wonders I must see——away, far away!

*'Beyond the fields we know' is a phrase borrowed from the work of
Lord Dunsany, one of my favorite tellers of tales.*

Ambrosia

APOLLO WAS TO blame. He was late getting to his sun-chariot that morning and took a slice of ambrosia along, to breakfast on as he drove his steeds across the sky. So it was a crumb, so slight a crumb, fell to the earth of mortals.

"It looks like honey," said Glaucus. He sniffed at the golden crumb. "Smells like it too. Sort of."

His wife was skeptical. "When has honey fallen from the sky?"

Glaucus was ever the sort to come up with a ready answer, whether sensible or preposterous. "Bees do fly," he said. "Perhaps a very large bee, a gigantic bee—"

This idea made Astyoche uncomfortable. The stings of bees of ordinary size were quite bad enough! She could imagine herself swelling up like a ripe pomegranate if stung by an enormous one. The woman warily scanned the skies above them.

"Hmmph." Only the sun, riding above the scattered clouds. For all she—or Glaucus—knew it could have fallen from there. Astyoche knew better than to mention that idea to her husband. Rather, she asked a practical question. "So, do you think this honey-stuff is safe to eat?"

"You could try it and find out for yourself," replied Glaucus.

"No, my fine husband, it would be better if you tasted it," came his wife's immediate reply.

At that very moment, a mongrel dog, both scrawny and scroungy, aimlessly wandered into their yard. Glacus watched as it sat scratching at fleas somewhere among its protruding ribs. "I know," said he. "We'll try some out on Hector."

The tiniest of pieces he broke off and held it out in his palm. "Here, boy. A treat for you." The mutt cringed at the voice and gave him the most suspicious of looks but finally came over, tail between his legs, to lick up the proffered food.

Hector sat back on his haunches and gave the pair of humans a long look, before saying, "My! I haven't felt this good since I was a pup."

"I didn't know you could speak," said the astonished Astyoche. Glaucus only stared, mouth agape.

"Neither did I. In fact, I don't know why I never did before."

"He's getting bigger," muttered Glaucus.

Yes, bigger, better looking—there was no denying it. His coat had grown thick and luxuriant, his tail curled most extravagantly. Now Hector eyed the chunk of ambrosia in his master's hand.

Glaucus was not sure he could keep this alarmingly transformed canine from taking it. "Into the cottage, woman," he hissed to his wife. "Quickly!"

Door shut and bolted behind them, Glaucus listened to Hector snuffling and scratching. Would those flimsy boards hold? He should have repaired them long ago. The whole house wouldn't hold up to any serious effort to breach its walls. There had never been any reason to worry about that as the couple never had anything worth taking. Until this morning.

"We should split it right now," stated Astyoche. "And don't you think of giving me a smaller piece than yours!"

Glaucus had been thinking of just that, to be sure. He looked at his wife's expression—and the heavy piece of firewood she had picked up—and rethought.

"Quickly!" she hissed. "The door is giving in."

Indeed, it was bowing inward somewhat more than it should. At once, he broke the crumb in two, as evenly as he could, and handed half to his wife. Both swallowed their pieces down.

"My, that warms one," said Astyoche.

"Doesn't taste bad either." It *was* something like honey but also something quite different. Glaucus couldn't quite put his finger on the difference and, moreover, he was distracted by the sudden changes in the woman he had married. She'd never been that tall!

He felt his own tunic growing tight and beginning to tear. He was further distracted when the door suddenly buckled and gave in. A wolfhound-sized Hector stood in its warped frame, cocking his head at the two. "So you've eaten it all, eh? Oh, well." The dog lifted his muzzle and sniffed. "Hmm, there seem to be several bitches in heat within a league or two. They won't be turning me down this time!" He wheeled and bounded away, howling heartily.

Glaucus's attention returned to his wife. Was that Astyoche? A goddess stood before him! He felt quite like howling heartily himself!

Let it be said the couple paid little attention to anything other than each other for the next couple of hours. "This makes up for the honeymoon," Astyoche finally declared. That had been a disappointment and she had never hesitated to let Glaucus know it.

He had similar sentiments but had known better than to express them. "I'm ravenous," he said. "I wonder where we can get more of that stuff."

Astyoche felt decidedly hungry herself. "I'd go for some normal food." There was little of that in their hovel. There was none at all a minute or two later. "There is always the pig," the woman suggested.

Glaucus was fond of their sow and, moreover, considered her an investment. It didn't feel right to eat her now. Maybe later. "I'd prefer some beef," he told his wife.

"The king has plenty."

That was all the encouragement Glaucus needed. He wheeled and headed out the doorway, his head crashing into the lintel. "Ouch! How did that get so low?"

"It is you who got so large, husband," Astyoche told him. She looked him up and down, rather appreciatively. "Oh, I don't think we have any clothes that fit anymore!"

"So who's going to complain?" he asked and set off toward the king's fields.

It is most unlikely anyone who saw two towering, nude

demigods pass by recognized them as their neighbors Astyoche and Glaucus. And none complained. To just whom could they?

The cowherds did not complain either when Glaucus threw a young bullock across his shoulders and carried it off. They were only slaves. Let the king's soldiers tend to this sort of problem.

Those, however, cowered inside old Nisos's keep, only peeping over the ramparts until the couple was a safe distance away. Then they sallied forth with a great deal of noise, clashing their spears against their bronze shields and bemoaning the fact that their adversaries had retreated, depriving them of their glory.

Nisos was not fooled. But that is a different tale.

Astyoche was busy barbecuing the rear half of the purloined bull—the front portion being saved for breakfast—when a tremendously loud buzzing began. She remembered her earlier fear of enormous bees and looked about with some concern. Sure enough, a great striped insect was descending toward them.

It alighted near the couple and transformed into a demure and not at all diminutive maiden. She still had gauzy wings attached.

"Hi! I'm Mellisa the Messenger! The Busy Bee of the gods!" She gave the pair a looking over. "We've gotten into some ambrosia, haven't we?"

"Is that what it was?" wondered Glaucus.

Astyoche had a more practical question. "Are we immortal now?"

"Oh, you need nektar too for that. Ambrosia keeps you youthful and strong and beautiful. Nektar makes you immortal. One without the other would be no good! Who would want to be stooped and wrinkled when they were only a million years old?"

"Better than being dead," muttered Glaucus.

At that moment, Hector came bounding out of the dusk, wagging his tail in a most satisfied manner.

"Oh, hello doggy," said Melissa, scratching him behind an oversized ear. "Are you a good boy?"

"Not today!" came Hector's cheerful response. He cocked his head, looking over her wings. "You fly? Do you know the big dog in the sky? I sometimes see her at night and wonder if she's lonely."

"Well, little dog, maybe you'd like to go up in the sky yourself and keep her company? You would be fed ambrosia every day."

The hound's tail wagged even more vigorously. "Sound good to me!" He turned an eye skyward. "I wonder if I can jump that high."

"No need," said Melissa, letting out a buzzy laugh. "I'll take you up later."

That, of course, is how the constellation we know as Canis Minor ended up in the southern sky, ever in pursuit of Canis Major or, as Hector calls her, the Big Bitch. He chased her so far she can't even be seen from Greece anymore.

"As for you two," she went on, turning her attention back to Astyoche and Glaucus, "I'm afraid you'll need to remain earthbound."

"Will this—wear off?" asked Astyoche.

"I'm afraid that, too, is so. Not quickly. Some effects will linger all your lives."

"Linger?"

"Yes. It has a long half-life."

Glaucus nodded wisely though he had no idea what a 'half-life' was.

"Well, come along, boy," called Melissa, as she turned back into a bee. Cradled in her six legs, Hector howled a goodbye and was carried away. It is doubtful he ever missed his former master and mistress.

Those watched the great insect dwindle and disappear in the sky. Astyoche turned to her husband. "We'll have to find a way of getting more, you know."

"Absolutely," he agreed.

The next morning they were noticeably shorter, though their old clothes still did not begin to fit. Moreover, they were unable to consume more than a quarter of the bullock for breakfast.

Neither questioned what their course should be. "Which way to Olympus?" asked Astyoche.

"North." And so they set out. The couple made good time at first.

"I'm not feeling as strong," complained Glaucus after a while.

"Me neither. Let's rest over there." His wife pointed toward a cave in the hillside. It looked like a pleasant-enough spot, with tall cypress standing about its entrance.

They might have known a well-tended cave was already occupied. A venerable centaur, white hair and beard hanging to his withers, greeted them. "Welcome, travelers!" He squinted at them, seemingly puzzled, before slipping on a pair of spectacles and squinting again. "I say, not quite the ordinary run of travelers, are we?"

Astyoche and Glaucus were astounded, having neither seen a centaur nor spectacles before. None the less, the woman announced, "We're off to Olympus to get ambrosia."

"Ah! So that's it. I thought for a moment you might be some sort of minor gods. Like my old buddy Hercules." Glaucus did not mind at all being compared to the heroic demigod.

"They won't let you in," continued the centaur. "The gods do not like to share. And—" He scrutinized the pair again. "I doubt you'll have enough left to get you to the top of the mountain anyway. You'd do better going to Hades."

The couple could only give each other perplexed looks at this advice.

"Time no longer matters in the underworld," explained their host. "Come on in and have some wine, won't you?" They followed him into the roomy but not overly tidy cavern. The horse half of the centaur apparently knew nothing of restrooms. "The effect of the ambrosia would not wear off. I think." He suddenly seemed doubtful. "Maybe there is something in my books."

There were a great number of those, stacked about the place. Neither Astyoche nor Glaucus could read, so they didn't set much store by what might be in them. As many others, they were suspicious of all things they didn't understand.

"Isn't there any way we could get more?" asked Astyoche.

"Oh, you could go where it is made." He handed each goblets. They were of gold, encrusted with luminous jewels, emeralds, sapphires, and each worth more than all the money either mortal had ever seen. That didn't interest them at the moment.

"Not on Olympus?"

"Doves carry it to the gods each day, from beyond the dawn." That sounded even further to travel than Olympus. The centaur noted their dejection. "They fly over here around noon. You might see one if you've a sharp eye."

Now they did have sharp eyes, at least for the time being, and could see much further than before.

"Also, you might smell it," said the old centaur. "It is quite fragrant, as you may have noticed."

"But how do we get one of these doves to land?" wondered Glaucus. His eye strayed to the powerful centaur bow hanging on the cave wall.

"Oh no, none of that my boy! The gods would be likely to strap you to a mountain top for the vultures to consume. Old Prometheus isn't the only one they've done that to, you know."

"I have a way," announced Astyoche. "Come with me, husband." With a quick farewell and thank you to the centaur, they were back out into the sun. It was still morning, but barely. They hurried to the top of the highest hill in the vicinity.

Glaucus sniffed. "They're near." Both scanned the skies.

At once, Astyoche began cooing. Surprisingly loud she was! Glaucus watched a curious dove descend toward them, growing larger and larger. And larger—it was quite enormous. As it hovered above them, trying to figure them out, he reached up and grasped a tree-like leg. "I'll hold it while you get the ambrosia," he called.

That was not to be. The huge gray bird began to lift him from the ground. Astyoche barely had time to leap up and wrap her arms around the other leg.

"Are you two going to hang onto me all the way to Olympus?" asked the dove.

"It looks that way," Glaucus replied. "Or you could set us down with a little of your cargo."

"I'd end up as a pigeon pie for Zeus if I did that. Just hold on, mortals. Or don't. I don't much care." It winged on toward the mountain of the gods, following the flock of its fellow columbine couriers.

When the great Mount Olympus stood before them, the doves rose, up and up, past its highest peak. "I don't see any sign of the gods' home," remarked Astyoche.

"They don't actually live on the mountain, humans," said the dove. "An invisible stairway leads from its summit to their world."

The line of doves had climbed into the clouds and disappeared from sight. Having been delayed by the couple, their own ride was the last. Now the birds descended toward a gleaming city, with lush green fields and forest lying about it as far as could be seen. Having a bird's eye view of it, that was pretty far.

"Best you just let yourselves be seen rather than trying to sneak in," spoke the dove, "Um, but you might get off me first so no one knows I brought you, okay?"

"Certainly," agreed Astyoche. "We've caused you enough trouble." She and Glaucus exchanged glances.

"That's most unlike you, my dearest," said her husband.

"It is, isn't it? I don't know what's come over me."

They did manage to slip unnoticed off the dove, screened by its fellows as they lit in a great colonnaded courtyard. A tall, statuesque woman was keeping track as each bird was unloaded by a group of scurrying fauns.

She took notice of them at once when they showed themselves. "So, stowaways? Which one of these bird-brains brought you here?"

"Beats me," lied Glaucus. "They all look the same."

"They do, don't they? If I asked them I could probably find out but it doesn't matter to me. And I have a schedule to keep." She checked off another load on her tablet. "I'm Hebe. I'm in charge of distributing the ambrosia."

"The nektar too?" asked Astyoche. She hadn't forgotten it was necessary for immortality.

"That's Ganymede's job." The goddess looked the two over. "Don't let Zeus see your woman," she warned. "She's somewhat attractive at the moment and that's enough for him."

Astyoche wondered where she could find Zeus and learn if it was true.

"You're somewhat attractive yourself," said Glaucus.

Hebe smiled tolerantly. "That's just the ambrosia talking," she told him. "It does make one horny at first."

"For the first couple thousand years," interjected one of the satyrs. All his fellows snickered.

"Oh, you guys are always horny. Take that load off to the nymphs now, will you? And don't dawdle."

"We never dawdle," one assured her.

"So complain the nymphs. Now, as to you two—how much ambrosia have you consumed so far?"

"Just a crumb," said Astyoche. "About this big." She held thumb and index finger an inch or so apart.

"And we shared that," Glaucus added.

"Ah. Not nearly enough to make you dependent. I guess I'd better report you to someone who can make an immigration decision."

"You can't?" They didn't like the idea of being passed along through the divine bureaucracy. They had some knowledge of the mortal version.

"I'm only the goddess of youth and spring. Ho, you," she called to a young woman in shining golden armor passing by. "Go tell your boss about this pair."

"Couldn't we have a little ambrosia while we wait?" asked Glaucus, in the most ingratiating tones he could manage.

The goddess gave him a firm shake of her head. "You'll have to talk to Athena first. If you're approved to stay, come back and I'll fix you up." Neither mortal appeared at all comforted by that assurance. "Don't worry, she's nicer than her reputation makes her out to be. Even if Zeus is known to refer to her as his headache."

"Is she, um, attractive too?" asked Glaucus.

"I would never say otherwise, remembering what happened to Paris! But she isn't into guys." Noting Astyoche's immediate interest, she said, "Or women either. Unlike Artemis."

They stood watching Hebe order her little workers about for a while. There wasn't much else to see in this big otherwise-empty courtyard. Both wanted to get out and explore Olympus! "Here she comes," said the goddess of spring. "Who's that with her? Oh, Hestia. That makes sense." She turned to them and whispered in an aside, "Both virgins, officially, but that's no more than an aspect of Hestia. She's as into guys as the next goddess, and always reverts to virginity, well, *after*, you know?"

"That must be handy," observed Glaucus.

How like a man, Astyoche thought. Losing ones virginity over and over was surely uncomfortable.

Athena was at least a head taller than her companion, who was plump and pretty. Not at all what either of them expected from a deity. "I'm disappointed," murmured Astyoche. "She's not wearing her armor."

This, the tall goddess of war and brains caught. "That would also be uncomfortable, little mortal," she said, her voice perhaps an octave lower than Glaucus's. "I only armor up when necessary."

Had she read Astyoche's mind just then? The woman tried to think of nothing and failed completely.

"That kyrtle dœs look comfy," commented Hebe. "So, both of you are going to decide on this?"

"It's Hestia's decision, ultimately," said Athena. "She's goddess of the hearth and home, after all."

"Unless my brother overrules me," said Hestia.

"Yes, Dad might do that. No need for him to know about any of it though, is there?" she asked. "I'm just here to give advice." Her gray eyes swept imperiously across the human couple. "It takes grit to make your way here. Some smarts too. I admire that."

"But they don't belong," commented Hestia.

"Yet they have tasted of ambrosia, right?" Athena looked to Hebe.

"A morsel," she admitted. "Not enough to matter. And I do not want to get involved in this!"

"What would we do with them?" Hestia asked her companion. "They'd need to have a place in Olympus. Jobs." Her gaze went to Hebe who shook her head vigorously. She wouldn't be offering them employment.

"They're only peasants, I think," Hestia went on. "You aren't slaves, are you?"

"No, ma'am," murmured Astyoche.

"We're free folk," spoke Glaucus, his voice only slightly more loud.

Athena nodded approval. "That's good. If you belonged to someone, we'd have to return you." She chuckled. "But not necessarily alive."

"Yes," said the goddess of the hearth. "We can't have you going back and spreading gossip about Olympus, you see. If we don't let you stay, we'll have to—well, dispose of you somehow."

"I suppose it probably will come to that," Athena intoned, with a great deal of gravity.

"Oh, you silly things," exclaimed Hebe, in frustration. She motioned one of the little fauns to her and whispered into its large hairy ear. It nodded and scampered off. "Come to my grove," she told them and marched away. All four, mortals and goddesses alike, followed.

At last Astyoche and Glaucus got a look at the wonders of Olympus. "It's like home, except better," Astyoche whispered to her husband. Across fields and hills of intense green, more vivid, more *alive*, than any they had ever known, they traveled.

In the distance, they heard the baying of hounds and glimpsed figures coursing along the edge of a great forest. "Who's that?" asked Glaucus.

Athena gazed toward them. "Oh, that's just Artemis and her girl-gang. Don't get in their way, little man. Her hounds would as soon tear you apart as a stag."

Perhaps this wasn't such a good place to be, after all, he thought.

Hebe's grove was just that—and more. There was a small house, or temple maybe. Astyoche wasn't sure which word one should use for a god's abode. Fruit trees bearing both scented blooms and ripe fruit. Deep, vibrant lawns, brilliant flowers scattered throughout. It was quite lovely, she felt. She wouldn't mind living right here.

"Maybe I could get on as one of her gardeners," whispered Glaucus. It seemed like a pretty good idea to her right then. They all seated themselves on the luxuriant grass, as soft as any cushion. The songs of birds sounded all around, more musical than ever they had heard, and the more distant maahs and baahs of sheep.

"What you need is some nektar," Hebe announced. She held up a hand of warning when the other goddesses looked ready to raise objections. A faun trotted up and handed her a stone jar. Hebe carefully allowed no more than a couple drops to fall into each of the two bowls she had ready. A little water was poured in with the liquid. "Just this much for now. The water will make it easier to drink down."

Hestia and Athena exchanged suspicious looks.

Down it went, both draining their bowls. Astyoche made a face. "It tastes like swamp water."

"Umm, yesss—" Glaucus's chin fell on his chest and loud snores began. A moment later, his wife slumped over on the grass.

"I take it that was *not* nektar," said Athena.

"Water of the River Lethe. I always keep a little on hand and always eventually find it useful." She looked on the two slumbering mortals. "I'll call Melissa to carry them home. I daresay all of this will seem like a dream when they awaken."

"If they remember it at all. Or anything! A little too much Lethe water can do that," said Hestia.

"I think I got the amount right. But the ambrosia they consumed will still have its effect on them. They won't be the same people they were before."

"That's for sure," agreed Athena. "It might be fun to keep an eye on them."

*

Astyoche opened her eyes. Whatever had happened to the door? It was hanging entirely off its hinges! She shook her husband. "Wake up, Glaucus!"

My, she didn't remember him ever looking so handsome. And vital. And interested!

She felt pretty interested herself. The two vigorously explored their interests for the next hour and some. When they rested, Glaucus said, "I had the oddest of dreams last night."

"Why, so did I, husband," answered Astyoche. "I do wish I could better remember them."

"Dreams are fine but I want to be awake right now. I don't think I've ever felt so awake and so alive. So ready to do something!"

"Me too. I think the future will be good. I *know* it will be." The two went to the off-plumb doorway and gazed out into the night.

Far above them, a little dog of stars ran across the sky.

GREENMEADOWS STORIES

A Dragon in Distress

SIR GRISSOL LOVED picnics. He also loved breakfast and so, each morning—weather permitting—he ate toast and marmalade on his front lawn.

Until, one Wednesday, his customary meal was interrupted by a dragon. It was a big, red one: wings, claws, fiery breath. Yes, the whole dragon package.

Now Grissol was a brave enough fellow, though, like all of us, not as young as he used to be. He brandished the marmalade knife, crying, "Back, bloodthirsty brute!" At the same time, he looked over his shoulder to gauge how far he was from his castle.

"Oh, is that lime marmalade?" asked the great crimson creature, settling down across from the knight. "May I?"

Sir Grissol nodded. As he watched his uninvited visitor devour toast, the old fellow tugged at his long white mustache in a thoughtful manner. "I understood that you wicked worms ate, um, damsels."

"Too much fat," confided the dragon. "I have to be careful with my diet; I'm pushing three thousand." He patted his ample midsection. "And it *is* hard getting into the air, sometimes."

"Oh, yes, I can sympathize with that." Grissol eyed his own waistline. "How I miss bacon!"

"But speaking of damsels," the dragon continued, "I have one in my cave, right now."

"Ah, dastardly dragon!" Some of Grissol's fire came back. "I might have known." He paused. "When should I come to rescue her?"

"It wouldn't do any good," sighed the worm. "She won't leave."

The old knight gave him a questioning look. "If you come with me, I'll explain. It's not far," assured the beast. "By the way, my name is Ransax."

"Pleased to meet you," mumbled the perplexed warrior. "Sir Grissol Greenmeadows, at your service."

Sir Grissol saddled his steed and set forth, with the dragon ambling along beside him. "Flying is so tiring," Ransax remarked, looking around. "This seems like such a nice, quiet neighborhood; I'd hoped to retire here." A sudden burst of smoke rose from his nostrils. "Then, Surrey came along."

"That is the damsel, I take it?"

"Yes," he replied. "You know, we dragons can assume human form, if we wish. But this shape—" He flexed his wings. "Is much more impressive."

Grissol didn't know but he wasn't about to tell the dragon.

"I'm not much as a human; just a fat, old man, and bald, to boot." He took a glance at Grissol's shiny head. "No offense intended."

"Quite all right, my good, uh, Sir Ransax."

"It's Lord Ransax, but you can call me Randy. Need a light?" The affable worm watched Grissol fumble with his pipe. "Anyway, this Surrey's got it in her head that she's in love with me and, worse, that I'm in love with her but don't know it."

"Some young girl? Sees you as a romantic figure, no doubt." Grissol bit down on his pipe stem. "I run into that sort of thing. Well, when I was younger, I did."

"Not quite the case, here," said Ransax. "Ah, we've reached my cave."

"Complete with angry villagers, I see."

"Surrey's relatives," explained the dragon.

"Here he is," bellowed one big, toothless fellow. "What's the idea of running off and leaving our Surrey?"

"You should be ashamed of yourself," an old woman chided.

Her companions nodded their heads at one another, murmuring their agreement and general disapproval of the dragon.

Ransax turned to his companion and shrugged. "I could eat a few, but then you'd try to slay me."

"Yes, I suppose I'd have to," admitted Grissol.

A plump, middle-aged woman came to the door of the cave. She bounded forward, arms opened wide, to embrace the embarrassed beast. "Dragon Dearie, you're home!"

"Um, yes, good day, Miss Surrey, and please don't squeeze so hard." The dragon belched. "It makes me build up steam." He turned to Sir Grissol. "Won't you come in and have a bite, Greenmeadows?"

"I'll whip up a lovely lunch for you," promised the dowdy damsel. "Now, you should really rest." She shook her head disapprovingly at the dragon. "He needs me to take care of him, he truly does!"

"My mistake," observed Ransax, as the pair entered his cave, "was to let her see me as a human. She will forever think of me as a helpless, lovable, old gent, rather than a mighty, if slightly over-the-hill, dragon." He led the knight down a passageway to his study. "And now," he sighed, "I think she's planning our wedding."

"The family seems to approve of her designs."

"They believe I have treasure piled away."

"Do you?" asked Sir Grissol.

"I'm comfortable." Ransax obviously didn't want to discuss the subject. "I hired Surrey as a housekeeper, but she's taken the job much more seriously than I intended."

"Why don't you simply fire her?"

"Far too late for that. All the folks around here are her relatives. If I told her to leave now, I might as well forget about a peaceful retirement. Assuming she *would* leave." He looked around the room. "I do so hate having to move, and I paid a fortune for this cave."

"Hmm." The old knight's face took on a crafty look. "I have a plan. One old bachelor may seem like a catch to your Surrey, but *two*—here she comes." The housekeeper entered with a tray.

"The Lord Ransax has invited me to live here with him. Make up a bed for me, will you?"

She peered suspiciously at Grissol and then at her employer. Ransax gazed at the rocky roof, as innocently as a dragon is able.

"Whoops, I do believe I've spilled my tea," lamented Grissol.

"No problem, old boy. Surrey will clean it up. Run along, love, and get the mop." Ransax had quickly grasped the plan.

The bewildered woman threw up her hands and left.

"Lend me your knife," requested the dragon. He began to trim his claws. If you think human toenails can be bad, just imagine a dragon's!

Surrey returned with a mop. "Ick! That's disgusting!" she shrieked, as a chunk of claw went whizzing by her head.

Grissol scratched his stomach and said "I feel like having a beer. How about you, Randy?"

"Excellent suggestion. Fetch us a couple, my dumpling."

"No, I won't. It's much too early," she scolded.

"We'll just have to go down to the cellar, then, and open a keg."

They locked themselves in the cellar all afternoon, playing rummy and telling stories of their younger days. If they heard Miss Surrey approach, they would break into off-key song.

The pair came up barely in time for supper. Surrey had placed a complete meal on the table, but the dragon dismissed her effort with the wave of a talon and demanded hamburgers.

"And quickly, if you please!"

The pair had time to down another bumper of beer (or was it two?) before she returned with a high-stacked tray and a sour look.

Ransax bit into his. "You burned it!" he complained.

"Mine's raw," grumbled the elderly knight. He nibbled some and then let it slip out of his fingers. "Oops," he said, and wiped his greasy hand on the table cloth.

"I've never seen two such crotchety, sloppy, unappealing old fellows," moaned the dismayed damsel, retreating to the safety of the kitchen until they finished their mess—and left her one to clean up.

Yet the housekeeper stubbornly kept to her perceived duty. Surrey was not one to be easily dissuaded, especially when such duty came attached to a reputed hidden treasure. She laid out their beds and went off to her own, convinced that tomorrow would be better.

The next morning, just as they sat down for breakfast, a shrill scream came from the bedrooms. A few minutes later, Miss Surrey came by, carrying her bag.

"That does it," she proclaimed, with a determined expression. "I hope the two of you are very happy together." Out the front door she went, never to return.

"What do you think decided her?" asked the dragon.

"She must have found that I kept my horse in the room last night," answered Sir Grissol. "He's not housebroken, you know."

So it was that the valiant, and decidedly devious, knight, Sir Grissol Greenmeadows, rescued a dragon from a damsel. Surrey found herself an innkeeper in the next county, who certainly made a better husband than an aged dragon. Ransax learned his lesson, and hired a butler the next time. And, once a week, he and Grissol would get together to play gin rummy and reminisce.

Room and Borders

"WHAT? A TOLL?"

The soldier looked thoroughly embarrassed. "Prince's orders, sir," he told Sir Grissol.

"And you'll have to pay me when you come back through," said the man on the other side of the turn-pike. "The king couldn't let Pitanga do this without retaliating."

"If your fat-headed king would just recognize the border had changed we wouldn't have this problem," claimed the Pitangan man-at-arms.

"Our borders are our borders," came the Carambolan's retort, "whatever ridiculous claims your petty prince may make." He shook his halberd in what he probably intended to be a menacing manner. His heart was obviously not in it.

"Now, now, let's not start a border war, my dear fellows. Tuppence to cross?"

"Plus a penny for the horse."

"Hmmph. I think I'll walk next time." Grissol Greenmeadows was never eager to part with his pennies. He handed over the required coins and led Battercap the rest of the way across the short span. The narrow River Acerola flowed dark and peaceful below.

"I'll have to have a word with our king when I get back home, Batty," he told his steed as he climbed into the saddle. "Hidalgus should know better."

Batty kept her opinion to herself, but had she spoken she would undoubtedly have told Sir Grissol he needed to lose some weight.

Fortunately, it was not far to the cave of his friend Ransax. Nowhere was very far in the realms of Pitanga and Carambola for they were quite small realms. Moreover, it was pleasant, open, rolling land. One could walk across the both of them in the course of a day and there were taverns along the way that made such outings worth the while.

To be sure, if one stopped at too many of those taverns the journey could consume more than one day. Especially if one consumed too much of their fine ale.

Ransax knew all about the dispute. That should surprise no one. Dragons like to keep up with all the gossip and more so when it might affect their pocketbook. Or their hoard, more properly.

"It's all about the Acerola changing course," the great red creature explained as they settled down among the disheveled shelves of his library. "It cut through a little oxbow upriver and Barbacuso claims that land is now part of Pitanga."

"And Hidalgus would dispute the claim. I know the man well enough to recognize that."

"The land, of course, is without value. Swamp."

"Well, maybe they'll see the foolishness of it in a while." Both knew, at heart, that was unlikely. But it didn't cost anything to hope.

It did cost to return home that evening. More than it had before. "Three pence?" Grissol asked the Carambolan border guard.

"The prince upped his toll, so we had to act, didn't we, sir?"

"Nay, it was the king who raised it first," objected the Pitangan soldier on Grissol's side of the border.

"Well, we knew you in Pitanga planned to do it, anyway. Oh, and another penny for your horse, Sir Grissol."

The knight wondered how soon that might go up as well. Not for long; the meat pie and flagon of strong southern wine awaiting him at home made him forget it altogether.

Mid-afternoon of the following day, Grissol was lounging on the lawn before his modest keep. Grissol named it a keep. You might call it a manor house. He put down the newly arrived copy of 'Shield and Steed' when he noted Ransax ambling in his direction.

It's hard not to note a ton-and-a-half red dragon, to be sure.

Even when its a red that has mellowed to a slightly brownish tone, like old claret.

"It's gone up again," stated the dragon, with no preamble, as he settled his bulk on the grass.

"Gone up? Oh, the toll." Grissol shook his head, causing his wide-brimmed straw hat to slide slightly askew. "Most inconvenient." He found it hard to feel very concerned at that moment. He didn't have to pay to go home like Ransax.

He removed the hat, wiped his shiny pate with a handkerchief, and replaced it before Ransax made any further comment.

"Half a shilling now. However—" A deep rumbling chuckle erupted from the dragon. "I explained that I was an animal so I should get the same rate as a horse. Tuppence, it cost me."

So that had gone up too. "It should be easy to go around, shouldn't it? Especially for a dragon?"

"When I was younger, I would have simply flown across the border. Not quite up to it these days." He spread his wide wings. "I could still manage to hop over the river somewhere, but I am rather easily noticed."

That would not set well with either ruler. They would send someone to demand the toll. The last thing either Grissol or Ransax would want is tax collectors at the door.

"And don't advise me to switch to human form. Either one of us would have to swim unless we went far out of our way."

"Hmm. A boat maybe? But that would be only a temporary solution."

"Dragons do not like to be fenced in," grumbled Ransax. "Give me room!"

"Yes," agreed Grissol, "lots of room. Without tolls."

"And all because the river changed its course. I'm sure it's not the first time."

"Been doing that every few years since I was a boy," said the knight. "Never bothered anyone before."

"Hmm. It would be interesting to see where it flowed in earlier days," mused Ransax. "There must be maps. We could show our lieges—"

"My dear Randy! That might just stir up more strife. I do believe you are mistaking Hidalgus and Barbacuso for reasonable men."

"Oh, yes, of course. I was thinking like a thoroughly sensible dragon, wasn't I?" The dragon pondered for a moment. "I suppose it isn't really about the river at all, is it?"

"The two have been rivals since they were riding stick horses on opposite banks of the Acerola and shouting insults at each other. I suspect the king still rankles over being called 'poopy britches.' It didn't help any when Hidalgus wooed and won Barbacuso's sister."

"Oh, the prince resents that?"

"No, Hidalgus does. And then, Barbacuso has never liked the fact that he is a prince and his neighbor styles himself a king."

"His realm *is* every bit as large. Maybe larger." There was a slightly steamy snicker. "Especially since he just added to it."

"Well, let's just hope it doesn't come to war. Terribly inconvenient. King Hidalgus would surely want me to round up some of the farmers and march off to fight."

The dragon gave him a long look. "I suspect, my friend, that with a few farmers, you could defeat either or both of our monarchs and rule yourself."

"What a dreadful idea. I consider myself thoroughly retired and intend to remain so." Grissol, it may be noted, was a fighting man. Or had been one, more accurately. Thoroughly retired or not, he knew of war as none of his neighbors did.

To be certain, so did Ransax. No whimsy was involved in his being dubbed 'the Rapacious' by men far and wide. Indeed, even other dragons sometimes used the epithet and they are notoriously hard to impress.

"I completely understand," said Ransax. "Hmm, the river. I say, Greenmeadows, I think I have an idea. Do you mind if I go nap on the cool stone floors of your dungeon a while? I think I'll need to be out and about tonight."

"It's a wine cellar, not a dungeon. I only imprison casks of port there and that's, um, for their own safety." He gave the dragon a suspicious look, wondering perhaps if his port would continue to remain safe. "But feel free."

Ransax didn't show himself again that day and in the morning he was gone. Grissol thought one of the casks sounded with an unduly hollow resonance when he rapped it. He was at tiffin when the news came.

"The river's changed course again," his steward informed him. "Overnight! Cut right into Pitanga's side this time."

"You're positive, Manuel?" There had certainly been no flooding. It hadn't even rained since Tuesday.

The man scratched his head as if digging for the answer. "I got it from my wife who got it from Farmer Muddles's wife. Muddles is dependable, sir, though I can't speak as to the wife." He looked to see if that went down well before going on. "His neighbor Digges had his cows down to drink early and saw it with his own eyes. There was already soldiers there, says he, looking it over and arguing. Soldiers from, um, both sides o' the river."

"Most odd," was the only comment the old knight was willing to make.

The next day, it seemed the Acerola had again changed its course, and in favor of Pitanga this time. "A whole swath of farmland," reported Manuel. "But there's still the parcel what was added to Carambola yesterday. No one's sure what belongs where now."

Grissol was willing to up his comment to, "Most extraordinary."

At dawn, the knight found a dirt-caked Ransax stretched on the

Greenmeadows lawn. "So," he asked, when the dragon opened an eye, "where did you move the river to this time?"

"Barbacuso's favorite tavern now belongs to Hidalgus." Ransax yawned. "I hope that's enough to make them see sense. I'm quite tired of digging."

Grissol had his doubts. His king called him to his side shortly after. The knight barely had time to finish his breakfast. But he did —Hidalgus was not going to prevent that, no matter how urgent the king's imagined need.

He also took the time to warn his steward not to allow any sheep to graze near Ransax. The dragon might be retired but he was not reformed.

A handful of baronets and ill-equipped knights had gathered, some bringing a retainer or two along. King Hidalgus was addressing them and pointing westward now and again. The monarch was tall and thin, with cavernous eyes, and a gray-streaked beard that reached nearly to the ground. He and the Prince of Pitanga had been competing as to whose was the longest every since both could shave.

Barbacuso's beard, what with him being a head shorter than Hidalgus, would drag on the ground unless he remembered to throw it over his shoulder. More than once had it slipped his mind and caused him to trip. Hidalgus secretly hoped he would be forgetful more often, though he wouldn't say such a thing publicly. His queen might hear of it.

"We'll show Barbacuso that we intend to keep the river as our border," he proclaimed.

Someone asked, "But, um, sire, weren't you arguing the opposite before?"

There were some gasps—it does not do well to remind kings of such things—but Hidalgus took no offense. "We must be flexible, my boy," came his affable reply.

Grissol could see now it was one of the king's younger sons who had raised the question. Prince Pedro. A good lad but probably not one with much of a future if he remained around these parts.

"We'll lose some good bottom land if we do that," came another voice. There were murmurs of agreement.

"Aye, nearly three acres. And *my* land!" spoke Squire Tallow.

Grissol decided to put in his two farthings' worth. "You won't be losing it, Tom. You'll just need to pay the taxes on it to Pitanga."

There followed an immediate—though short—hush. It seemed this had not occurred to any of them.

"Ha! True indeed, Greenmeadows! So why I am I here wanting to fight anyone?"

"Yes," one of the knights said. "The border moving dœsn't hurt any of us."

Hidalgus was having none of this. "It hurts me," he stated. "And I can hurt you."

There was no arguing with that logic. "I command you all to show up here at the castle first thing tomorrow with your men. We'll march to the river and have it out with the Pitangans!"

The group dispersed with little enthusiasm. No one wanted to fight on a summer morning. But might not the men of Pitanga be preparing to march too? They couldn't allow that.

Grissol slowly rode the half-league back to his manor, giving himself time to think. Battercap was grateful for the pace but the knight could come up with no ideas. He explained the situation to Ransax over flagons of ale.

"So. I must do a bit more digging. I'm too old for this, especially in the chill of night!"

"Now, now, Randy, these are the mildest of summer nights. You didn't complain about sleeping on my lawn."

"Well, the water's chilly anyway. And it is hard work."

"To be sure, my friend, to be sure. Are you willing to give me a clue as to your plans?"

"Just be at the river with Hidalgus." The great worm rumbled a laugh. "If you can find it."

He could not. When the Carambolan contingent arrived at the banks of the Acerola the next morning, the Acerola was not between them. Just mud. Hidalgus glared across it at Barbacuso and his men.

"It seems," observed Sir Grissol, "that there no longer is a border. That is, if we insist the river marks it."

Ransax sauntered up to the Pitangans on the far side. "This is a dilemma, isn't it? I say, do you suppose the river got tired of your bickering and moved away?"

The two rulers looked at each other across the empty river bed. "You don't believe that, do you?" called Barbacuso.

"No, of course not," came Hidalgus's reply. "Still—"

"Maybe Acerola would come back if—"

"We just agreed to let her be the border, wherever she flows."

They both thought on that no more than a few seconds. "Done," cried Hidalgus.

"I agree," called out Barbacuso. "Return, river, we implore you!"

Ransax had ambled across the stream bed to stand beside Grissol. "It will break through the earthen dam I threw up in a bit and come roaring back," confided the dragon.

Sure enough, in a few minutes they heard the rumble of its flood. The men on both sides cheered as the water churned past them.

And from that time on, River Acerola was accepted as the border, regardless of where her whims might lead her to flow. Peace returned, save in the hearts of the two monarchs.

However, both Hidalgus and Barbacuso found the money they had been making off their tolls too welcome to give up. "We'll keep it to a penny," proclaimed the King of Carambola. "We're not greedy, after all."

"And a farthing for each animal—which dœs *not* include dragons," added Prince Barbacuso, rather pointedly looking at Ransax. That was quite unnecessary, as he was the only dragon there.

"I suppose it's an acceptable price for getting things back to normal," he mused. "But I hope you're the one doing most of the visiting, Greenmeadows."

Sir Grissol Greenmeadows didn't mind that. His port would be safer.

Doctor Agon

FAR AWAY AND long ago there lived a king. His father and his father's father had been kings before him. It was the family business.

This king, whose name was Johannes, had no son. He did have two daughters. They were large, sturdy girls, for they came of large, sturdy parents and the large, sturdy people who had come to rule their land both by the strength of arms and the strength of their own arms. The princesses were named Carolina and Catarina, and few could tell which was which, for they were twins.

Normally, finding suitable husbands for two healthy, strapping, and decidedly royal girls would have posed no problem. Indeed, suitors were plentiful and the princesses liked each better than the one before. There was even the son of a duke, all the way from France. "We should hold out for an actual duke, rather than a younger brother," Catarina told her sister.

"Damn right," agreed Carolina, who was inclined to salt her language just a bit. "And one at least as tall as us."

Catarina, ever inclined to be agreeable, nodded but she wouldn't have minded a short suitor, were he a real duke.

King Johannes's dilemma came from the fact they were his only heirs. One would be queen and, though ruler in both name and fact, her husband would surely play some role in governing. Or wish to play a role, which might be worse.

And which was the older? One girl had certainly been born before the other—Johannes could not picture them both popping out of his Queen Mary-Ambrosia at the same time—but no one was certain which came first. The good queen, it may be noted, complained enough about their size appearing one after the other.

Suitors came and went but one was persistent. That was Ludwig the Prudent, ruler of the kingdom next door and better know to his people as 'Old Penny-Pincher.' It was no secret King Ludwig had long had designs on his neighbor's kingdom. Marriage certainly required less effort and expense than war. And he could get gifts for the princesses wholesale. He knew someone.

Ludwig had a wife already but claimed that would be no impediment. Wives were easy enough to lose. Why, he'd done it a couple times already!

"Mary-Ambrosia, my dear," said Johannes one day. "Something must be done."

"Of course," she murmured, her attention all on her embroidery. The queen embroidered large and bold. Some said that was the warrior nature of her ancestors. Others whispered it was her over-sized and clumsy hands.

"It would not do at all to marry Carolina to Ludwig. Or Catarina, for that matter. When the other chose a husband, there would surely be conflict over the throne."

"Yes, dear. You could always divide the kingdom."

Johannes was quite taken aback by that suggestion. For some reason it had not occurred to him. He mused on it for the better part of a minute. The stupefied look on his face told Mary-Ambrosia he was thinking deeply. But no— "And have one half fight the other? No, no, that's not good at all. I need a clear heir to my throne."

"But how do we choose one daughter over the other?"

Indeed how?

*

When one can't decide, one seeks advice. Then, to be sure, one must decide whether to follow that advice. To make matters worse, Good King Johannes convened a council of the wisest men of his kingdom and would have many words of advice from which to choose.

Fortunately, it was a small kingdom and not noted for an abundance of wise men. The king found not one suggestion to his liking. Certainly not that he order his darling daughters to battle to the death. Likewise, he rejected the idea that he institute polygamy in his realm and marry them both to the same man. Johannes suspected the fellow with that bit of advice had his own eye on a prospective second wife.

"I must cast a wider net," he confided to his prime minister.

"Certainly, sir. Shall I draw your bath?" It being a small kingdom, the minister did double duty as butler.

The thing, King Johannes decided, was to call upon professional advice-givers, learned doctors and philosophers from the cities and great universities.

There came the philosopher Mediocrates, self-styled gadfly of the University of Saragossa, where oft he disputed with he who held the Chair of Magic, only once being turned into a toad. Restored he was, at the Chancellor's insistence, but some claimed there was but little difference.

While the bald and lump-like philosopher had journeyed from the sunny south, the next to arrive came from a cold land beyond cold seas. That was the renowned scientist and astrologer, Professor Hawkinstein. He had been joined in France by another philosopher, Sartracus, the famed Egg-essentialist.

Hawkinstein traveled in a comfortable palanquin; the philosopher disdained any such bourgeois conveyance and chose to walk. It was said, though, he would frequently perch on the rear of the ox cart conveying their luggage.

Last to arrive was Dr. Agon, from far Pitanga. His lateness was largely the result of his concerns about the fee he was to be paid. Agon was as famous for his way of holding onto a florin as for his scholarship.

The doctor reputedly had retired to a cave—a quite comfortable one—in the countryside. He was a stout old man who wheezed some. There were those who claimed they actually saw a little steam come out of him from time to time. This seemed most unlikely to Johannes, though he kept an eye open for it.

The four savants observed one another warily when called before the throne. The king's herald—who also served as wine steward—stepped forward to introduce them. "From the Institute of the—is that Sorbonne, sir?" he asked, trying to make out the words on his scroll.

"Sorbet. We make the finest in Paris!"

"Ah. Very well. I present the renowned philosopher Sartracus."

The impossibly tall, skinny man, wrapped in a shabby black robe, stepped forward, peering at the assembly through owlish glasses. "All existence is a bird!" he proclaimed. "It hatches, demands to be fed, then flies away."

"He wishes he could fly away," commented Dr. Agon. "His mistress nags him even worse than Mediocrates's wife."

An odd, high pitched laugh came from Hawkinstein. "We had to sneak out of Paris so she wouldn't know where he was going."

The Egg-essentialist glared at them as the herald continued. "From Spain, the learned Mediocrates. I say, isn't Saragossa near the Ebro? There are some fine wines coming out of that region."

Johannes thought he would like to know more about that, even if it were irrelevant, but they received naught but a scowl in answer. "I cannot teach anybody anything," the scholar stated. "I can only make them think they learned something."

"Yes, very well," said the king, seeking to be agreeable. "Perhaps we'll, um, think we learned something, eh?" He turned his eyes with some eagerness to the herald, silently beseeching him to continue.

"From the University of Esox, the famed Doctor Hawkinstein. That's in England, Highness."

"That it is. The only land worth living in, I must say," came that same strange voice. The king might have taken umbrage at this rudeness had he not been distracted by the fact that Hawkinstein was not speaking. The words came from a small black bird perched on his shoulder. The doctor himself reclined in his palanquin, gazing into space and apparently thinking deep thoughts.

"And to round out our guests—" This statement remained

unfinished for at that moment a diminutive woman pushed her way into the room. She spat her cigar out on the floor and mashed it underfoot.

"A sorry lot," she said, looking over the assembled wise men.

"We invited the six greatest minds we knew," protested the prime minister. "We were fortunate these four chose to make the journey."

"You should've invited the second six. You're more than fortunate now I'm here."

A deep sigh came from Sartracus. "Majesty, might I present Madame de Buveur?"

"Mademoiselle," she snapped. "And don't you forget it."

"I like her," whispered Carolina.

"I don't," replied her sister, "but I hope she can get us husbands."

"We welcome you, Mademoiselle," said Johannes, wondering if she would ask the same fee as the others. "Pray continue, Otto, er, my herald."

"I present the noted historian, Dr. Agon," said the man.

The king peered at the fat old fellow. "Yes, yes, I believe we have some of your books in our library. Retired now, I understand?"

"Indeed so, your highness. I have traveled widely in my long life and now crave only the comfort of my country home."

"His hole," snickered Sartracus.

"A hole of my own, which none of you wastrels can afford," came Agon's reply.

Unexpectedly, a trumpet blared outside the chamber's door. This was played by one of Johannes's two court musicians. He employed a violist too but his instrument was not so well suited to fanfares. "His majesty, King Ludwig of Toadflax!" announced the herald, though all could see who it was striding into the room.

Ludwig—Ludwig the Third, more precisely—also came of large and sturdy people. That some of that largeness had settled around his belt must be admitted. His full blond beard hung almost to that belt, but it was not quite full enough nor long enough to hide his paunch. "What's this foolishness, Johannes?" he bellowed. "Just marry one of your girls to me and have done with it!" His voice reduced to a hiss. "I intend to rule Liverleaf, one way or another."

"Are you invading, Ludwig? You'd better bring an army next time," came Johannes's retort. It is to be admitted that his temper had increasingly frayed and now was coming apart at the seams.

"Hmmph! Maybe I will." The visiting—or invading—king winked at the twins. "One of you had better be ready to greet me. Or both!" Throwing back his head and laughing loudly, he wheeled and left the castle of King Johannes.

"This Ludwig seems a bad egg," remarked Sartracus. "One would not wish to be yoked to him."

"Ah," came Mediocrates's rejoinder, "but he who is not contented with what he has, should seek what he would like to have."

De Buveur's frown was undoubtedly meant for each and every man in the room. "Why should the princesses marry at all? Let them rule!"

"Isn't that up to the young ladies themselves?" asked Agon. "You do want to get married, don't you?"

Two heads nodded vigorously.

"You see, all women want to marry, ma cheri." Sartracus could not hide the petulance in his voice. "I don't know why you keep turning me down."

"Then you don't know me!" she sniffed.

Mediocrates stroked his unkempt beard thoughtfully. "The unexamined wife is not worth wedding. Hmm, maybe you could permit me to make some examinations, mademoiselle?"

The Egg-essentialist glared at him. "There is only one day, Monsieur Gadfly, always starting over, but if you keep that up you may not see it come again."

"Indeed? I'd like to see your calculations on that," spoke Hawkinstein. Or his bird.

"It's a figure of speech, good sir," explained Agon. "Have you any thoughts to add to our deliberations?"

For the first time, the scientist himself seemed to actually be present, pondering the question. It was, however, the black bird that squawked a reply. "Decades of research have led me to conclude all the universe is made up of *things*. I call this 'Thing Theory.'"

Johnnes nodded impatiently. "Yes, yes, but what has that to do with our problem?"

"Is a problem a thing?" asked Dr. Agon.

"Hmm. I'm not sure. Let me return to my equations." It is to be assumed he did. Hawkinstein did return to staring into nothingness.

"So, dœs anyone have a practical suggestion?" asked Queen Mary-Ambrosia, who was becoming peeved with her husband's handling of this council.

"I would propose a competition," spoke Agon. "The winner chooses one of the princesses as his wife and becomes the heir."

"Or one of us chooses him," added Carolina. Or was it Catarina?

"Ah, splendid," said Johannes. "Let us adjourn and consider what sort of contest it will be overnight. Dœs, um, Mademoiselle de Buveur need a room? We would have to open the east wing."

"I am afraid," announced Sartracus, "she came to stay."

*

"You have an idea for a competition, sir?" asked King Johannes. "And couldn't it have waited until the morning?"

The historian shrugged his rather massive shoulders. "It could but I thought it best to get things moving. Best to explain it in privacy, too. I suggest slaying a dragon. Or, more properly, facing one."

"But where would we ever find one?" wondered the king. There hadn't been any in the neighborhood since his father's time. That one was only migrating and rested awhile on the hill across the valley.

"Allow me to show you. It might be best if your highness left the room," said Agon to Mary-Ambrosia, as he began to disrobe.

"Um, perhaps you should, my dear," felt Johannes. "And just what are you up to, my good doctor?"

"No way," stated the queen. "If we're paying this fellow I intend to get our money's worth!"

"A woman after my own heart. I need to demonstrate something to you and don't wish to ruin a perfectly good wardrobe in the process."

That seemed sensible to the royal couple. Why that velvet doublet was barely worn at all! Mary-Ambrosia rather liked its midnight blue coloring and the neatly done embroidery. She did not so much like the sight of an increasing amount of Dr. Agon's flesh. There was rather too much of it.

Both were shocked and amazed when the corpulent scholar at last dropped his breeches. No, no, not that—Agon had a tail. Short, but a tail none the less. Then he began to slowly change, change from a man into something larger, something scaly. A few minutes later a decidedly massive dragon crouched in the middle of their antechamber.

"So, a revised introduction is in order, isn't it?" asked the creature. "I am Ransax. When I was young, some named me 'Ransax the Red,' which is not very imaginative." Dr. Agon—Ransax—was indeed a quite red dragon. "I was partial to 'Ransax the Rapacious,' but was entirely willing to be addressed as Lord Ransax. Now my friends mostly call me Randy."

"Fr—friends?" asked the Queen.

"Yes, human friends, your highness. Dragons are not inclined to make friends with each other. We're far too covetous of each other's hoards."

"I hope you're not interested in my hoard!" exclaimed Johannes. "It is exceedingly small."

"The agreed upon fee is quite adequate, majesty." Ransax let out a steamy chuckle. "In the old days I would have dropped from the sky and collected my fee in a very different manner."

"So," said Mary-Ambrosia, ready to get down to business, "you intend to fight the girls' suitors?"

"Surely not to the death!" Johannes added.

"Consider it more a test to see how they do in a crisis. A confrontation with a dangerous dragon!" His grin revealed many long and rather sharp teeth. "Not me. I'm too old and fat for that sort of thing. Yes, even as a dragon." He patted his ample midsection. "I can call one of my young relatives here to do the job. That's why I wanted to get started."

Ransax looked toward the window. "I am greatly tempted to take a flight and get some of the kinks out of my wings," he said. "Best I change back." This he began at once, noticeably shrinking, the wings diminishing, the tail shortening.

"This is something dragons can do, sir?" asked Johannes. "Change to human form?"

"Indeed so. If you had read those books of mine reputed to be on your library shelves, you might know this."

King Johannes of Liverleaf decided he would go to the royal library at his first convenience.

Dr. Agon seemed to be back to his human form, aside, to be sure, from the tail. Neither the queen nor king was likely to forget its presence, now matter how well it might be covered up. He began pulling on his clothing. "Actually," he told them, "I'm not much of a flier these days. Too heavy. Once I might have flown off and found a suitable dragon for you." He snickered. "But I would have been a suitable dragon myself then, wouldn't I? I can send a message and get him here by, oh, maybe tomorrow night."

Fully dressed, he bowed to the royal couple and exited. Young Klymax would be just the dragon for this, wouldn't he? Ransax had already told him to be ready for something.

He was a great one for schemes in any form.

*

"Things are not always what they appear to be!" Dr. Hawkinstein suddenly announced. Neither he nor his bird had spoken since yesterday's council.

"Indeed so, sir, indeed so," murmured Agon.

"That," further explained the professor, "is because things are made of things."

"But of what," asked de Buveur, "are those things made?"

Hawkinstein at once went blank-faced, apparently returned to his calculations. They heard nothing from him and his spokes-bird the rest of the day.

The visiting savants were, of course, invited to view the coming trial of the suitors. There was little else for them to do in Castle Liverleaf but sit and argue and drink Johannes's wine.

Sartracus was on his second bottle and de Buveur was helping him progress toward a third. The mademoiselle, despite her apparent animosity of the previous day, had also apparently spent her night with the philosopher.

"If you're lonely, seek bad company and go get drunk," proclaimed that philosopher.

Mediocrates sat down with them. "The unexamined wine is not worth drinking. Allow me to examine that bottle more thoroughly, my colleagues." That he had already examined a bottle or two seemed more than likely.

Sartracus filled the Spaniard's goblet. "We are our choices in wine," he said.

Mediocrates winked at de Buveur. "And in women?"

"I make my own choices," she snapped.

"Ah yes, we are big on free choice. We can be the chicken or the egg!"

"But then who comes first?"

"I'd better," stated de Buveur, draining her goblet. "I demand my freedom to be first!"

Sartracus hastened to agree. "Yes, of course. Freedom is what is done to us—is that right, ma chere? I sometimes get it confused!"

"Sounds right. Right enough. Fill me up again."

"Ah," said Mediocrates. "The only true wisdom is in knowing what you know!"

"But sometimes happiness," added Dr. Agon, "comes in not knowing what you don't know."

*

The suitors for the hands of the royal daughters assembled in the early morning light. Five in number they were, in an open courtyard overlooking the valley.

Alas, the French nobleman had gone searching elsewhere for a shorter bride, but an Italian aristocrat had filled his place—the Conte di Cibella from Piezo, the city famed for its towers that leaned so far they all fell over. His ancestral palace had been among them and he sought a new home. The conte was a scrawny, pot-bellied fellow with more hair on his chin than his head, and a threadbare wardrobe.

When it came to titles, he was outshone by Pedro, a younger son of the king of Carambola. Prince Pedro outshone no one in other respects, being notable mostly for being unnotable. He had been too shy so far to even speak to Catarina, much less Carolina.

There was Bratislav Wurst, scion of a wealthy Bohemian merchant family. His father had ordered him to bring a bride with a title back to Prague. It would be good for business. Brat didn't mind, not being fond of girls. One would be as bad as another. His eyes occasionally went to the pair rounding out the group of competitors.

Those were the brothers Ulmus and Sorbus, two soldiers of fortune from Riga, just returned from warring with the Cossacks. The pair were big, swaggering fellows, with bristling mustachios. Long swords swung at their sides. Why they thought themselves suitable suitors, no one was sure, but Johannes had been timid about turning them away.

"I like this land," said Ulmus, looking out across the hills. "It goes up and down."

Sorbus agreed. "Very flat where we come from. Better for riding horses!"

"Oh, all the horses here have longer legs on one side than the other, for going around the mountains," Pedro informed him.

Both Letts nodded gravely at this bit of information.

"I have a brother named Kosax," Dr. Agon confided to the king. "I don't think that pair would want to go to war with him. It's his boy I got to come here to help us."

"Um, that's good of him, sir. Does he, um, expect payment?"

"I may give him a little something from my fee. He's just here to blow off a little steam. Literally." Agon chuckled and maybe blew off a little steam himself. "Klymax is a youngster yet at an hundred and twelve, and up for a bit of a lark."

"I hope it proves to be no more. I say, what is this?" There was a commotion by the gate. A moment later, Ludwig marched toward them, an attendant at his heels.

"I don't think much of his army," commented Dr. Agon. He did notice, though, the king's man carried a blunderbuss.

"Did you think you could leave me out of this, Johannes?" bellowed the bellicose monarch. "Not that it matters who wins your little game. I'm marrying one of your daughters regardless!"

At that point, the philosophers straggled out into the courtyard. It was far too early and they were far too hungover to say anything at all, much less anything interesting. Professor Hawkinstein still seemed to be in another world but his black bird turned a bright eye to the proceedings.

"All here then?" began Agon, brisk and businesslike. "Our suitors over there. Everyone else out of the way." He cocked an eye at the king of Toadflax. "Which are you, your highness?"

Ludwig hesitated a moment. "With me," he told his attendant, and went to join the suitors. There were some murmurs of disapproval but the doctor made no comment.

"So," he announced, "here is your test."

The sound reminded Johannes of laundry flapping in the wind. A great number of sheets. He quickly realized it was the beating of two great bat-like wings as a huge red dragon rose above the parapets.

The Conte di Cibella promptly fainted. Bratislav crouched behind the Latvian brothers. Ludwig's man turned and ran. Ludwig watched him go for a few seconds, turned his eyes back to the monstrous worm, and hastily followed him to safety.

Ulmus and Sorbus slowly backed away, swords drawn but seemingly in no hurry to engage Klymax. "Stop cringing back there, Brat!" growled Sorbus.

"You're in our way," added Ulmus. "In case we have to retreat some more."

The dragon rose high above them and then rather gracefully dropped to the cobblestones. Its wicked head went back and forth, glaring at the remaining men. Before he knew it, young Herr Wurst was in the open and the Letts were behind him.

"Not worth it," stated Ulmus.

"Agreed," said Sorbus.

Then Bratislav was completely by himself. Not long, as he bounded toward safety.

That left Prince Pedro of Carambola. He looked Klymax up and down. "Well, you're quite a magnificent fellow," he said. "I do believe I might know a relative or two of yours."

A deep chuckle erupted from the dragon. "It is possible, your highness."

"Call me Pedro." The young man looked about. "I think I must have won, huh?"

Cheers began to rise, a few at first, then most of the crowd. "Prince Pedro! Prince Pedro!" came their cries.

"Give me that," growled a livid Ludwig, grabbing the blunderbuss his attendant held. "And quit yelling 'Prince Pedro.'" He strode toward the young man, leveling the gunne as he approached. That was most foolish, for he completely neglected the dragon standing near by.

A few seconds later, only the royal legs protruded from Klymax's maw. A few seconds after that, Ludwig the Third was no more than a name in the history books, and one that rarely rated more than a paragraph.

"I see," commented Mademoiselle de Buveur, "one is not born, but becomes, a dragon-fighter."

"Liberty!" cried out Sartracus. "Down with all kings! Down with the bourgeois order! Oh, my apologies, majesty."

"Quite all right," said Johannes. "We all became a bit stimulated. My daughters included." Catarina and Carolina were making their way toward Pedro, a bit cautiously as Klymax still sat there, apparently carrying on an amiable conversation with the prince. A steamy belch or two punctuated his speech. Johannes and Mary-Ambrosia followed in their wake, with Dr. Agon ambling behind.

"He's a nice guy," said Carolina, "but not really my type."

"I think he's just fine," rejoined Catarina. "Brave, and well-mannered too. If you aren't interested, he's mine!"

Queen Mary-Ambrosia turned around and gave Agon a long

and somewhat suspicious look. "You had something to do with this outcome, didn't you?"

"Well, your majesty, Carambola is right next to Pitanga and the young prince might have met a dragon or two in the past."

"Yourself included, I dare say."

"Indeed so."

"Oh, I say, Johannes, is that creature turning into a man?"

Klymax was doing exactly that. A minute or so later a large, naked, and rather impressive young man stood there. Yes, he did have a tail.

"Oh, I want him, Daddy!" cried Carolina. "He's *perfect!*"

"But dear, he's not, well, human," objected Johannes.

"He can be quite human as long as he wants to be," said Dr. Agon. "And I might point out that there is an empty throne next door that he could now occupy."

"Well." The king thought on this. "What do you think of this, young, um, man? And what should we call you?"

The dragon-turned-human took a look at Carolina and grinned. "Sounds great to me. Call me Klaus. King Klaus of Toadflax! I like that."

"Me too," said Carolina. "When's the wedding?"

*

As Professor Hawkinstein and his bird announced, before departing with their fee, "Things change."

Klymax became a king, a human king, and took the throne of Toadflax, with Carolina at his side, and Prince Pedro married Catarina and one day they occupied the thrones of Liverleaf. Both couples lived happily for many years after, though not quite forever.

To be sure, King Klaus did not age as quickly as his Queen Carolina, and one day left her, flying off toward the high distant mountains. Not however, without leaving several large and sturdy children to carry on.

Fair Games

Two ELDERLY GENTLEMEN strolled beside the river. The bald but sprightly fellow with the long white mustaches everyone knew; Sir Grissol Greenmeadows was a legendary adventurer in his youth and a voice of reason in his old age—a voice his liege, the King of Carambola, frequently needed to hear.

The other man, portly and bearded, was a mystery to many. A very few knew this was the human form of the retired dragon Ransax, who owned a commodious cave in the Principality of Pitanga. Greenmeadows spoke only of him as his friend Randy.

"I'm glad there is no jousting at this fair," said Randy. "Knights with spears always make me nervous."

"Don't care for 'em that much myself. Leave fighting to the battlefield, I say, and find more enjoyable forms of recreation." His eyes lingered on Dame Amanita as she passed by.

"Women are the most dangerous recreation of all," opined Ransax. As most dragons, he avoided the opposite sex except during mating season.

"But worth the rewards, my friend! Even when one loses the game."

"Hmmph. No one wins that game. The wise quit when they're ahead. Or not too far behind."

Sir Grissol only shook his head. "There are dragon sports, I would assume."

"To be sure. When I was young I would enjoy a bit of one-on-one air hockey. The idea is to keep the, um, puck from hitting the ground. That's a point for the other dragon."

"Puck?"

"Oh, we would use whatever was handy—sheep, knights, boulders. We'd toss them around for hours, though some hold up better than others. Once a sheep has been spiked into the ground it's pretty useless."

Grissol preferred not to ask about knights. Even in full armor, he suspected they would soon need replacement.

Two other not-so-old gentlemen strolled toward them. Both these were quite well known for they were the respective rulers of Pitanga and Carambola, which lay on either side of the river. They styled themselves friendly rivals but anyone could tell they were most unfriendly. On this one day of the Fair, the two must be civil to each other.

Each had a long, ground-brushing beard. They had been competing to outgrow each other's whiskers since they were in their teens. There was still no clear winner.

This was a day they did hope to name winners. Hidalgus and Barbacuso took great interest in the competitions between the citizens of their realms.

"Your highnesses," Grissol greeted them. Strictly speaking, perhaps, the Prince of Pitanga did not qualify as an 'highness.' It was better not to chance slighting him.

Hidalgus of Carambola returned the greeting. They were ambling along his side of the River Acerola so that was proper. "Lord Ransax. Sir Grissol."

Barbacuso mumbled something similar.

"Enjoy the fair, gentlemen," Hidalgus went on. "It promises to be a good day for Carambola." Prince Barabacuso scowled at that. "By the way, Ransax, I appreciate what you did for my boy Pedro."

"He's a good lad," said Ransax.

"That he is," agreed Barabacuso. "Takes after his mother." By which he meant Queen Styrfreya, who just happened to be the prince's sister.

Grissol felt the boy took after no one in either family.

"Always a welcome visitor at my cave," the dragon went on. "Glad to help him get settled." He bowed to the monarchs and both pairs passed on their ways.

"Settled far from here," he confided when they were beyond earshot. "With a good wife and a crown awaiting him."

"He's one man who won the game of romance," observed Grissol.

"Maybe so. At least the first round. Is this a game being played here?" There were two crowds of peasants at either end of a grassy space. Someone in the group to their left shouted out, "Red Rober, Red Rober, send beer to the sober!"

Two men in long red robes raced across the field with full foaming flagons. "It seems to be," ventured Sir Grissol. "What the rules might be I've no idea." If there were rules. "It might just be an excuse to drink beer."

"Since when have the men of either realm needed an excuse?"

"Giles spilled more," a voice called out. "A point for Pitanga!"

"It *is* an excuse to drink beer," noted Ransax. The man and the dragon strolled on.

Other games were played all about them. A group of youngsters were engrossed in Roll Out, rolling each other down a hill and betting on whether they would end up on one of the black or red blankets spread at the bottom. If they rolled off onto the green grass it didn't count. A tournament of Parmesancheesi attracted older—but just as avid—players. Vendors wandered through the crowd, loudly hawking their wares, trinkets and treats.

Some of the treats ended up being used in a game of Biscuit Ball between two packs of unruly children. The object seemed to be to pelt each other with them. Nearby, a rowdy group of teenagers played Smear the Peer. They took turns chasing and piling atop whichever lad wore a paper crown. The boys were decidedly enthusiastic about both smashing and smearing. Especially as young ladies happened to be watching.

Grissol had already been an esquire at their age. That position had provided him with more effective means of impressing girls.

"They say we're all even," a passerby commented to his mate. "Them Pitangans are tougher 'n they look."

"We'll get 'em in the next game. It should be a drinkin' game. Carambolans always win those!"

Out in the field ahead of them, a group was playing Spin the Tail on the Donkey. The donkey was being most recalcitrant about this, refusing to allow his tail to turn clockwise. "It's sorcery!" claimed a man in a robe that might have once been white. "The Carambolans have bewitched the beast."

"Right," groused another. "They've put a spell on the old fellow so his tail only goes the one way."

"I assume," whispered Randy, "that Pitangans and Carmabolans want it to turn different directions."

Grissol nodded. "And the poor donkey doesn't want it to spin at all. That's Brother Rencoro complaining, isn't it? He always finds something."

The man suddenly stood up straight, raising his arms to the sky. "No more cheating! I call upon the demon of sports!" he cried out. "Great N'ca'a, attend us!"

"Not again," someone sighed.

"Every time!" said another.

"Rencoro is an amateur wizard," the knight confided to Ransax. "He just has to summon something every now and again."

An odd figure was taking form before their eyes. Its most striking feature was its black and white stripes. And its head, which was a great shiny whistle. It whistled loudly now. "Anyone who doesn't quiet down goes in the penalty box," it declared.

"Penalty box?" whispered Ransax.

"It's wearing it on its belt. Never goes anywhere without it."

The dragon eyed it. "I don't believe I'd fit."

"You might be surprised."

"Hmm. I believe I'd just as soon not find out."

The demon N'ca'a went over to the donkey and tickled its rear with a grass stalk. The tail spun clockwise. "No penalty! Resume play!"

Brother Rencoro at once jumped up. "That ain't right, sir! They were obviously cheating!"

"N'ca'a's decisions on the field will not be questioned! To the penalty box!" With that he stuffed the man, long robe and all, into his box. There were subdued murmurs all around but no more complaints.

With that, the demon made the rounds of the ongoing games, blowing his whistle and assigning penalties as he saw necessary. Very rarely did anyone else see them necessary but that did not seem to bother him. "There gœs all our fun," Grissol heard, and, "We might as well head home."

Maybe he and Ransax should go as well, he was thinking, when the two monarchs moved far too purposefully in their direction. No chance to dodge them.

"We're ahead," declared Hidalgus of Carambola, "and there's just one game to go."

Barbacuso scowled. "You're only up one point."

"So you could end in a draw?" asked Ransax.

Both scowled now. "No one wants that." Hidalgus turned to his rival. "Let's make it a two of three sort of thing so I can beat you soundly."

Barbacuso seemed to be thinking this through. He brightened suddenly. "Oh, I could win, I mean, Pitanga could win overall if we take all three. You're on, Hidalgus."

"So what is this final contest?" asked Ransax. Grissol knew already.

"Tug of war. And we want you two to captain our teams."

That, Grissol had not known. "Surely you'd want younger men, your highnesses. We're not going to add much muscle."

"But plenty of weight," Prince Barbacuso pointed out. "Now, let's get to it."

They slowly got their teams sorted out. Some of the men weren't sure which country they belonged with, this late in the day. Eventually, a score grasped each end of the stout rope, with Grissol and Ransax in the anchor positions—as far from the mud puddle between them as possible. Each had quite independently decided to let go if they were pulled anywhere near it.

So there was groaning and growling and pulling and straining for a few minutes before the Pitangans slowly began to slide forward. It wasn't much longer before the first of them reached the mud.

"Carambola wins the first round," announced N'ca'a. There was cheering and more beering. Grissol made sure to wave to Dame Amanita. This was his own opportunity to impress girls.

Barbacuso was close to complete defeat. Even he could recognize that. "There's no rule we have to use the same teams for the next round, is there?" he asked.

Hidalgus only laughed. "I'm all right with it. You've already had your best men beaten."

"Then I challenge you to make it women against women this time."

The King of Carambola considered it only a moment. "Why not? There's no chance we can lose now." He gave N'ca'a a sidelong look. "Any rules against it?"

"None. But it will have to be all women on each side."

"Looks like we can sit this one out, my friend," Grissol told Ransax. The dragon only nodded and went off to confer with his prince after a while.

Something was banging inside the penalty box. N'ca'a glanced down at it. "Another twenty seconds," he said. "Are our teams ready?"

They were, and looked every bit as sturdy as the contestants in the previous round. Strong farm girls, stout serving maids and cooks, grabbed the rope and pulled with their combined strength and weight. This time, it was the Carambolans who were finally edged into the mud.

Sometime during the struggle, Brother Rencoro had been released, seemingly none the worse for wear. He did complain of a sore back for several days thereafter. "Cramped in there, it was," he complained to any who would listen.

Hidalgus was unhappy but he was still ahead. The best his rival could manage was a draw. However, just to be safe, he insisted, "Men again this time."

Barbacus smiled. "All my contestants will be male."

And Ransax would anchor the team—as a dragon. He had transformed while the women contended and now strolled onto the field.

"Hey, yer bringin' in a ringer!" someone complained.

"I assure you, sir, I am the same Ransax who pulled a few minutes ago."

"Will you allow this?" Hidalgus demanded of N'ca'a.

The demon gave the dragon an up and down perusal. "It is indeed the same individual. And he is a citizen of Pitanga, is he not?" Both monarchs nodded, one smiling gleefully, the other more morose. "He may play."

"Must we let him get away with this?" Hidalgus hissed in Grissols' ear.

The knight was afraid they would have to. The only solution would have been to find another dragon dwelling in Carambola— one as fat as Ransax.

The conclusion was never in any question. So they were still tied for this year's championship.

A loud whistle split the air. "Overtime!" declared the Demon of Sports.

"What? There's nothing wrong with a draw," sighed Grissol. "It's honorable."

"And people do want to go home," Ransax added.

"Anyone who tries to leave gœs in the penalty box," threatened N'ca'a. Some had already slipped away. Too late to penalize them.

"So what do we play?" came a voice from the remaining crowd.

"How 'bout Cotton Bowling?" someone answered.

"Or a foot race to our houses!"

N'ca'a looked about, trying to pinpoint the offender.

"May I suggest a Tan Fan match?" spoke up Sir Grissol. "I'll play for Carambola and Ransax here will represent Pitanga."

"Tan Fan?" asked the demon. "I, um, am a bit rusty on the rules."

"No problem. We are experts." He gave Hidalgus a sly wink. "Do our monarchs approve?"

"To be sure," said the Carambolan.

Barbacuso looked confused but his brother-in-law jabbed an elbow into his ribs. "Agree, fool, or we'll be here all night."

"Oh, yes, yes. Let them play, um—"

"Tan Fan, my liege," said Ransax. "Shall I deal?"

"By all means. Do we have two and a half decks?"

"Indeed, but I couldn't find a chess board. Will checkers work?"

"In a pinch. A hand for me, a hand for you, a hand for the idiot."

"And one folded in the middle of the board," added Ransax.

"Blue Stu!" cried out Grissol.

"Ah, but two eights and a four make Green Jean," Ransax pointed out.

"Only if the idiot plays it."

"This is like Black Jack?" asked N'ca'a.

"Never heard of it. Three twos. You'll have to throw them over your shoulder. No, the left one."

And so it progressed, cards played, cards withdrawn, cards turned into tiny flying darts.

"White Knight."

"Oh, very good. That's what, six and a third points?"

"Added to the negative four, that puts me in the lead."

"Ha! Orange, you lose," crowed Ransax.

65

"Why?" wondered the demon.

"Because nothing rhymes with orange, of course."

"Unless it's a Purple Orange," Ransax pointed out.

"Oh, quite so. Ha! Tan Fan!"

N'ca'a peered at the cards. "But didn't you have this hand before?"

"But there were a pair of sixes in play two deals back," explained Ransax.

"I'm playing my mild card," stated Grissol. "Nothing we've done before counts."

"Aiee! Enough. I declare this game a draw." With that, N'ca'a disappeared.

Hidalgus was simply glad the day was over. Barbacuso was still trying to puzzle out the rules of Tan Fan.

The Descent of Dragons

"BEFORE MAN, WAS the race of dragons. Not formed were they, like men, in the image of the gods, nor were their minds like those of men.

"In those days—"

"Just how long ago was this?"

Ransax looked up from his volume, his annoyance obvious—to those who knew dragons. "Millions of years, I'm sure."

"Millions?" objected Sir Grissol. "Surely the world hasn't been around that long!" He noted his scaly friend's expression and decided to drop the subject. "Well, go on."

"In those days," continued Ransax, settling down again to his reading, "only wild beasts roamed the earth. And the gods said, *Let us raise up the beasts, so they might know us.*"

"You say this is a holy text, Randy?" asked the old knight. "I always thought you dragons were a rather, well, skeptical bunch."

"Indeed," replied the dragon. "That does not mean we haven't our traditions. Though," he added, with a slight, steamy chuckle, "we may not take them quite so literally as humans do."

"Hmmph. I do believe that might have been intended as an insult."

"You are what you are." Ransax shrugged, his wings stirring up a faint breeze in the study. Dust wafted from atop the high, disorderly stacks of books.

"Our holy texts are repositories of dragon wisdom. And," he added, "often pretty good stories. We dragons do love stories."

Grissol Greenmeadows gave him a knowing smile. "This is one human who has learned not to take *your* stories quite so literally. I realize you like to, um, embellish."

"Perhaps, a smidgen," admitted Ransax. "But back to the *Draconotheca.*

"Many were the creatures they shaped, creatures of the air and of the sea and of the earth. Then of the stock of the weasel and badger, creatures that dwell in the earth, fierce, cunning, they created the dragons."

"So you're actually a—a weasel?" gasped the knight. "Everyone thinks you're reptiles!"

"And we usually do not attempt to disabuse them of the notion. Or we eat them before the subject comes up. But after all, Greenmeadows, do I truly seem very lizard-like? I'm not exactly cold-blooded, after all!"

"Well, I had wondered about the ears," admitted Sir Grissol. "Never seen a snake with ears."

Ransax pricked his large fox-like ears. "The better to hear you with, my friend."

Sir Grissol chuckled. "That's a good line. Someone should use it in a story."

"I suppose so. Anyway, your folk tend to confuse us with the wyverns, who *are* reptiles. To our eyes we seem nothing alike but then you humans all look much the same to us. Incidentally," added Ransax, "the gods formed your race of the apes. It is rather obvious to my people that they didn't raise you very far."

"At least we left our trees," huffed Grissol. "You still live in a hole in the ground."

"Ha, quite true, my friend, quite true. I admittedly can't see you climbing a tree."

Grissol, for a moment, recalled a much younger version of himself doing just that. Ah, the apples that grew in his neighbor's orchard! And his neighbor's daughter who might be found there as well—hmm, no need to mention any of that to this dragon. "So, you were raised up from weasels and we can claim the monkeys as our ancestors. Did the gods mess about with any other animals?"

"There is something about that in here," replied Ransax, leafing through his tome. "Not much though, as I remember. This book concentrates on my own people." He stopped and peered at a page. "Ah, yes. There were eagles. Or maybe hawks? It's a bit unclear. And the dolphins, of course. In other words," said the dragon, looking at his companion over the top of the out-sized book, "one intelligent race for each of the four elements."

"Dragons are fire, right?"

"No. Earth. You sun-loving humans are the People of the Fire."

"I suppose that makes sense," admitted the elderly knight. With a chuckle, he added, "I could be pretty hotheaded as a youth."

Ransax was still poring over his text. "Yes, eagles. It makes sense that they would have to be fairly large to be more than bird-brains." He shut the *Draconotheca* and placed it atop a tall stack of books. "I shall have to sort these out someday," he mused. "Speaking of descending, I just received some new barrels of Saragossan wine. What say we go down to the cellar and sample it?"

"I thought this was a cellar," said Grissol. It *was* downstairs from the living quarters, wasn't it?

"I have cellars below cellars below cellars here, my friend," claimed the dragon. "After all," he added, with a wink, "I have to hide my treasure somewhere."

Grissol Greenmeadows snorted. "I keep hearing of this treasure but I've never seen any of it." He rose from the overstuffed chair and stretched. "But I'll settle for seeing some of your wine right now."

"Bring along a lamp, will you? I know you humans don't see that well in the dark."

Lord Ransax led the way, down a dim hallway and then a stair. "We dragons tend to be secretive about our hordes. In the blood, you know?" he told the knight, with a slightly embarrassed air. "I'll admit I sometimes go down and sleep on it. It's a bad habit but it is something my people do."

"Sounds deucedly uncomfortable to me," opined Sir Grissol. "And cold."

"Dragon bodies tend to heat up any space they occupy rather quickly," replied his host. "Lying on a cool pile of gold can actually be quite refreshing. Ah, here we are." He pushed open a heavy oaken door. "Hmm, I thought I locked that after the delivery."

Stacks of barrels and racks of bottles lined the walls of the chamber. It was a well-stocked wine cellar indeed and the knight felt a twinge of envy when he thought of his own few small casks of port.

"The new stuff is over here." Ransax shook his head. "That barrel shouldn't be on its end. Monsieur Biber's delivery men know better than that."

"Biber, eh? I can't afford to deal with him." Grissol ambled over to the barrel, marked 'M. Biber,' meaning to put it onto its side— and perhaps sample it. It tipped over readily on its own. The loose lid fell off and rolled across the stone floor. "I say, this one is already drained!"

Ransax looked into the empty keg and sniffed suspiciously. "There was a human in this barrel." His long nose wrinkled. "Or I think it was a human. Slightly odd scent to it."

"An intruder?" asked Grissol. "Ah! Your treasure!"

The dragon immediately turned and started for the doorway. "Follow me," came his curt order. To the right and down stairs hewn from the stone they hurried, Sir Grissol huffing at the exertion of keeping up with the dragon. He had never seen this part of his friend's lair, nor even knew it existed.

Nor had he ever seen the dragon so focused. "I can still catch the scent," growled Ransax. "Definitely headed for my treasure chamber. Watch your head."

The rough rocky tunnel was too dark for Grissol to see any ceiling. Not by the light of the little oil lamp he carried. He reached upward and couldn't touch it. More of a concern for the dragon, maybe. Ransax halted and looked back at his companion.

"He's seen it now, and knows the way. I suppose I should eat him." He gave Grissol a sidelong look. "You would have to go all knightly on me, wouldn't you?"

"Afraid so, old boy. Can't have you eating people in my neighborhood."

"Well, here we are." There was no door, only a hole in the rock. This was all natural cave down here, Grissol suspected. He held high his light.

With a great foghorn of a bellow, Ransax sprang into the chamber, only to stop short.

"Why that's no man!" exclaimed Sir Grissol. Before them stood a somewhat diminutive dragon. Diminutive beside the impressive Lord Ransax, that is, who approached a ton and a half in weight. Other dragons, naturally, could recognize that Ransax was fat and old, but to human eyes he was simply *very* large.

This dragon scaled at maybe a third of that and was several feet shorter. "Draubax?"

It hung its head and murmured, "Hi, Grandpa."

"So you were in that barrel. And in human form?"

"Yes, sir," admitted the young worm.

Grissol knew dragons could do this and had seen Ransax as a rather disreputable-looking fat old man on a couple occasions, but had never been there for the actual changing of form. He wondered briefly whether the dragon was just as weighty when it was human. That would have made for a decidedly heavy barrel!

"I sneaked into the winery and hid," continued Draubax. "I—I wanted to see your treasure! I'll have a pile like this someday!"

"Ha, you'd probably like to steal mine, boy!" Ransax thundered.

The young dragon cringed. "No, sir, no! I wouldn't think of it."

"Don't be silly," his grandfather told him. "Of course you would. You're *supposed* to! That's what we dragons do."

Grissol Greenmeadows, meanwhile, was quietly surveying the

glittering heap of treasure. "As untidy as the rest of your place, Randy," he stated.

"I know exactly where every coin is," came the reply. "And if any are missing—" Ransax gave his grandson an exaggeratedly menacing look, before whispering to Grissol, "Were that another dragon he would not leave here alive. But Draubax is family. From one of my daughter's litters."

"I know where it is also, now," observed the knight.

"That dœsn't worry me. The butler knows his way down here too. I trust him to be discreet. I tend to be secretive with humans just on general principle and with dragons on long experience."

He turned back to the other dragon. "It is bad enough, young fellow, that you know about my treasure now. What is worse, I am short a butt of wine!"

"It was only a puncheon," Grissol observed.

"Well, it still quite a lot of wine," fumed Ransax. "Wine I paid for!" He regarded the young dragon for some time, apparently pondering. "So what do I do with you? Lock you up down here?"

"With the hoard? He might enjoy that."

The great dragon started to snicker. It grew into guffaws. "Indeed he would! Well, come along upstairs, boy, and we'll think about this."

Draubax quietly followed them back to the library. There, his grandfather suddenly demanded, "Show me your human shape!"

The young dragon eyed Grissol. "In front of *him*?"

"Think of him as family. Your dear old Uncle Grissol."

Said uncle harumphed rather loudly. Draubax simply shrugged and slowly began to change, growing smaller, bat-like wings becoming arms, tail and nose shortening. It took a few minutes before a chubby teenage boy, fairly normal aside from his stub of a tail, stood before them.

Ransax looked him over. "Very well. Until I tell you otherwise, you will remain in that form, my boy." His voice became a couple tones lower and decidedly more menacing. "And you'd better behave or I'll cut off your tail!"

The lad gasped. In a whispered aside—one the dragon-boy could undoubtedly hear—Ransax told his friend, "He wouldn't be able to return to his dragon form till it grew back. In a decade or two. It's sort of our connection to our other self.

"Greeves," he called. "Come in here, will you?"

The butler entered at once. He gave the naked boy but the slightest of glances. "Sir?"

"The lad here will be staying with us a while. Fix him up with a room, will you? And see if you can find him some clothes." He turned back to his grandson. "Hmm, you should have a human name, shouldn't you? Ever use one?"

"No, sir." Draubax might have seemed offended were he not already so cowed.

"How about Drab?" suggested Grissol Greenmeadows.

"Splendid! Drab you are."

"Do I have a say?" asked the newly-named Drab.

"Absolutely not. Now run along and do what Greeves tells you."

"That was interesting," commented Grissol, once the two had departed. "Always wondered about how you changed. Ha, I guess I still do!"

"Most understandable, Greenmeadows. You see, we don't change in quite the sense you're probably thinking. We keep our alternate forms in, um, what you might call another world, and switch them out. What looks like a transformation is really one body going away and another coming.

"Hmm. That actually makes a sort of sense."

"Don't I always make sense?" inquired Ransax.

Grissol ignored the question. "Other worlds, eh? I say, do were-wolves do the same sort of trick?"

"They do, indeed, except in their case the wolf demon already existed in another world and became entangled with a mortal human."

"Oh! Hmm, could you cut off their tails to cure them?"

"Dœsn't work quite the same way, I'm afraid. Now what am I going to do with that dragonling? I can't let him go spreading stories about my horde or how he tricked me. And I don't much want him living with me, family or not."

"Your daughter's boy, you say? Dœs this mean you had a wife at some point?"

"I still do. We mate for life but can not stand to live with our mates for very long. So we visit from time to time. During the mating season, of course, but also we sometimes simply miss each other and our families." His sigh might have suggested he missed that family right then. Or it might have meant something else entirely. "I should probably let them know where Draubax is."

"Drab, you mean."

"Drab, indeed. It can wait. Annex should keep a better eye on her boy but I remember well how rebellious young dragons are at that age. That's why a fair number don't get past that age."

Sir Grissol had a feeling Draubax might not if he spent much time in the cave of his grandfather. "How about letting him come and stay with me a few days? Get him out of your hair, so to speak. Or scales."

Ransax gave him a most skeptical look. "Are you sure of that?"

"How much trouble could he be?" At once he told himself it was a stupid question. Teenage boys, whether human or dragon, were, well, teenage boys. "I'll make him my esquire."

"That's rather impetuous. But so be it."

"If young Drab is willing," Grissol added.

"Whether he is or not," came the dragon's reply. "Greeves! Get that boy in here!"

An hour later, the unwilling Drab walked beside Grissol, who led his horse. He had found the dragon-boy had no idea of how to ride, nor how to do much of anything human. Rarely had Drab been beyond the mountains and the company of other dragons. Greeves had found him a kilt and blouse, both at least three sizes too large, and a straw hat for his big round head. The hair on that head was thick and black. The face below it was sullen.

But he was beginning to take interest in the things they passed, despite himself. Women, in particular. They continued, neither in any hurry, to the River Acerola, the border between Pitanga and Carambola, and the wooden toll bridge spanning it.

"So who be this?" asked the man at the turn-pike, giving the boy a friendly but curious look. Strangers were far from common. Moreover, the lad would be something to gossip about later at the tavern.

"My new esquire, Master Drab. I say, dœs he get the children's rate?"

The soldier shook his head. "Too big. That'll be tuppence for the both of you and a farthing for Battercap. Not making old Batter carry you today, eh? I reckon she appreciates that."

There might have been a veiled comment on the knight's ample midsection in that but he chose to ignore it and led boy and horse across. Stepping onto solid ground, he told Drab, "We're in the kingdom where I live now. It's not far to my keep."

"Then we're not in Grandfather's country anymore? What's it called?"

"Pitanga. But you're definitely not beyond his reach." He noted the sobering effect that had and went on. "You may be ignorant of most things knightly—or even human—but I think you are an enterprising lad. The way you got into your grandfather's cave is evidence of that!"

For the first time, Grissol saw a smile on the boy's face. "It was a pretty good trick, wasn't it?"

"It would have been if you'd thought it through and had a way to leave his cave."

"With his treasure!" Drab beamed at that thought.

Grissol didn't think much of it. An irate Ransax would not make a good neighbor. Drab was looking at women again. Girls this time. From the corner of his eye, he watched a pair pass them on the path.

"I've never seen a girl up close before," he said, perhaps a bit wistfully. "I wonder how they look without their clothes."

"You're not the first." Apparently, along with a human form went a human nature and a human interest in the opposite sex. "You know, they were looking at you too."

"They were?" He might have puffed out his chest just a bit.

"They were. I would recommend you not show them your tail, however. Here's my place. Greenmeadows Manor."

Drab politely avoided being critical of the little manor house. "I'll, um, live here? For a while?"

"If you wish. There's really nothing to stop you from changing back into a dragon and flying away, is there? I mean, Ransax might be peeved at your disobedience but he wouldn't go after you."

"And cut off my tail?" The boy smirked. "I don't think so. It might be best to keep Grandpa happy though. For a while, as I said. Are there girls here?"

"There's an whole kingdom full of them."

"Good," said Grissol's new esquire, and followed him in.

The Edges of the World

Stone

EACH MORNING MEDUSA combed her snakes before a brazen mirror. They could be quite unruly, writhing out of place as soon as she thought she had made some order of them.

"Who'ssss going to look at you?" they hissed at her.

"I shall," was ever her reply, and she went on arranging the serpents. Deep in her soul, she wished there could be another.

But all the men who came here wanted to kill Medusa. Some sought the glory of it, some felt a duty to slay a monster. Some wanted to use her head and its stony gaze for their own purposes. She had a parlor full of them, all turned to statues. Sometimes she rearranged them, from boredom, and placed them in compromising positions.

A very few were handsome and she might let out a sigh when her eyes went to their forms. Mostly the gorgon ignored them. She was too used to their presence. They were but so much clutter now.

And imagination only took one so far.

She was feeding her hair mice one evening when another intruder blundered his way into her cave. Night seemed a favored time for these heroic misadventures; perhaps the warriors felt they could accomplish their deed under the cover of darkness. Medusa lit several braziers until the place was as bright as noon. This man would see her and see her well. For a moment.

Ah, he was using the trick of a well-shined shield to reflect her image, so he would not gaze upon the danger of her eyes. Others had attempted this and ever made a mistake at some point. They might lose her image in the reflection and, without thinking, look about for her. They might be distracted by her other weapons, for

Medusa did not slay by sight alone. Let them try to keep their eyes on their shields while she loosed arrows at them!

Here he came. Oh, so comely a fellow, with his lithe body and muscles and very little covering them. He grasped a long leaf-bladed bronze sword and kept his eyes firmly on the round shield.

Then he halted. "Why, you're beautiful! I expected to glimpse a hideous monster."

She was glad he had made no comment on her snakes. These writhed in agitation at the moment. "Kill him!" they murmured, and "Petrify him!"

"Hush," she whispered. "So why do you wish to slay me, mortal man?"

"For the glory!" He chuckled in a slightly embarrassed manner. "That's what I told everyone. That or 'because she's there.' Really, I thought your head would be useful."

Medusa nodded. She appreciated honesty. There was much to appreciate about this fellow, she thought, as she looked him up and down and up again. Her gaze lingered around his middle.

"I'd rather you stayed with me a while." Medusa smiled at the thought.

"So might I," he admitted. The warrior kept his eyes fixed on his shield. From fear or admiration? she wondered. A little of both would be fine.

"But what would you tell those who expected you to kill me?"

He pondered this question for but a moment. "I'll just tell them I chopped off your head and, um, lost it while flying over the sea. I came here on a hippogriff, you know."

"Not the first," she told him. "Here," she said, picking up one of her scarves. "Use this as a blindfold and you'll be in no danger." She chuckled herself. "Not from my eyes."

There might have been a moment of mistrust but he took another look at her reflection and acquiesced. "I guess I'll have to work by touch," he joked. A little nervously, she felt. That was to be expected but she'd do her best to put an end to any doubts.

"The best way," she answered. But she was glad she could see him by the ruddy, flickering light of the blazing braziers. She wanted to—no, she should be the polite hostess first. "Are you hungry?"

"Only for you." That was all the gorgon needed.

She did need to let him sleep eventually. By the dying illumination, Medusa allowed her eyes to feast on the slumbering hero beside her. Her serpents stirred drowsily, before falling back into sleep. She should in a few minutes, but he was so good to look at, so handsome.

And it was so good to have someone with her. Someone who was not made of stone. Long had she yearned for this.

In the morning, he was already awake before her, his hands groping for her. That was what had awakened her, wasn't it? The snakes hissed a bit in protest.

Medusa slid out of bed, and looked at the long sharp sword and shining shield propped against her wall, just below the fresco Apollo had painted for her. It wasn't so good but one did not insult a god nor his handiwork—that sort of thing had gotten her into trouble in the first place. She hadn't always had this snaky head, after all. "Come to me," she called. He rose and embraced her willingly, avidly. As their lips met, lingered, her hands went to his blindfold and pulled it up.

"Best to be safe," she told the mirror, sitting down to comb her serpents.

The Sea-Wolf and the She-Wolf
a song

The She-Wolf met the Sea-Wolf
down at the edge of the tide;
said she, come live in the mountains
and ever run by my side.

Nay, board my outbound vessel,
said he, and be my bride;
and together we shall voyage
across the salt-sea wide.

My masts, they were once forest,
tall trees that sought the sky;
now they spread the canvas wings
that allow my ship to fly.

And fly it may, she said,
but not to yon peaks high;
to æries of the eagle
far above the seagull's cry.

The wind that drives your ship
was born in those heights,
it howls through long-lorn valleys,
as I do, moon-filled nights.

Ah, but that wind may bear us
to new lands and new sights,
where golden cities rise
and bazaars of unknown delights;

their burnished spires' beauty
no heart can scarce stand.
Think you not, asked she,
my mountains are yet more grand?

The She-Wolf left the Sea-Wolf,
where ocean met the land;
the Sea-Wolf sighed and turned
to cross the empty sand.

Whelp

ZARGAROTH LOOKED UP from his manuscript. "Carrying another mortal whelp, are we?" he asked. "How many is this for you?"

"I lost count centuries ago," came the flat, emotionless reply, "though this is the first in many years. Men do not call for us as once they did."

"They've stopped believing you succubi exist," said the arch-demon. "And from what I've heard, human women are doing your work for you quite nicely these days."

"Amateurs," spat Mepathet.

Zargaroth sneered. "All you know you learned from them. Even the shape you wear to allure men. Now, let's get the thing out of you."

"It is ready. I gave all of myself to it I could, so it would grow the quicker. It hurt."

"Yes. It was your duty to do so." Everyone hurt here. "I suppose you thought of getting rid of it."

"Every second. I know better than to flout the master's will in this."

He nodded his tricorned head. "Even to think it is dangerous. But inevitable."

The demoness nodded as well. "I have wondered why he does not gather the by-blows of the incubi."

"Those born of mortal women belong to the mortal world. We have no claim on them."

"Ah. This I did not know."

"And it will make no difference to your existence. Knowledge is just another burden for us. It mocks our impotence."

"All things do."

"Yes. Would there were an end to things. Would there were an end." It was almost a sigh and almost a curse.

That was what their master worked for. Both knew this and it was the only knowledge truly worthwhile. An end to suffering. An end to existence. He had promised this eons ago, in the times before time was.

"It is kicking at me," noted Mepathet. There was no emotion, no judgment, only a statement of fact.

Zargaroth laid a clawed hand on her belly. "A lively one. Whence came his seed? A strong man?"

She gave only a weary shrug. "They all seem weak, those who call to us." The demoness gazed down at her swollen body, pondering for a moment. "This one seemed more curious than lustful. He had no sense of being sinful. Most are racked with guilt over their falling." A mirthless laugh erupted. "Falling as did we."

"Such amoral men have fallen already. He had no need of your body to lure him."

"I was called. I must go." She had no enjoyment of her trysts. She could not even savor the corruption of men's souls. Not anymore. All was the same gray meaningless existence she cursed. The pain of being.

"Three days?" asked Zargaroth. Mepathet nodded. That was normal for a succubus' pregnancy, if she put all the resources of her body into the whelp's development. It was painful but it was best to be rid of the thing as soon as possible.

"Then let's remove it." He cleared his throat and spat a small flame into a corner. "Without damage."

That needn't be said. Their master required it. "It is attempting to expel itself," Mepathet said. She could feel it, a sharper pain than the dull ache of having the thing within her. Would that she could resume her old demon form. It would make things easier but she had so long worn the shape of a mortal woman that it had become who she was.

Zargaroth knew how to get it out. Not without pain, to be sure. What cared he for the pain of another succubus? He had midwifed for uncounted, uncountable, demon mothers over the millennia.

Tentacles curled from his wrists, probed, wrapped themselves about the thing inside her. "It comes," he stated.

A moment later, a fat brown mortal boy was grasped in his talons. Almost tenderly, he placed it on the table of polished black stone.

Mepathet gazed at the little thing. The whelp of that mortal man with whom she had lain. The man meant nothing to her. But this creature—it was of her. She couldn't feel anything for it, could she?

"It will make a fine treat at the master's table," said Zargaroth. "Leave now."

Dully, Mepathet nodded her head and went to wait again to be called.

The Book, the Beast, and the Burglar

IN A RED leather book—*what? No, I don't know what beast supplied the leather*—as I said, in a red leather book in the loftiest tower of Hirstel, a city of lofty towers, were written the names of all the demons of the lower planes. There, well-warded, it lay in the highest room of that tower, rising above the palace of Piras Tindeval, Prince-Sorcerer.

Hirstel, where all men are wizards, and all the cats, and most of the dogs, as well, was ruled over by Tindeval. His book of power had much to do with that. He kept it in a casket of silver, with the sign of Sebuchax thereon in gold. When the book was needed, the prince climbed the long stair of his tower and coming into the room—with due propitiation of the demon Qu'orthseth—he took it from its casket and read the names therein. Thus did he remain sovereign in the City of Sorcerers.

There was a young beggar, Im, who owned only castoff and broken spells. He was undoubtedly the weakest wizard within the five city walls of Hirstel, unless one counts some of the dogs and several of the rats. Rodents have never taken well to magic, yet some must attempt it.

His poverty was no fault of his own, but could be traced to his father, who had lost his only truly valuable enchantment by gambling with a small and treacherous feline. There is little doubt that a cheating spell was employed in their game of three-penny, but it was impossible to prove. Moreover, the corrupt judges of Hirstel ever favored the winner, however he came by his success. So, the unfortunate man lost his post as garbage collector, as he no longer had a demon helper to carry any and all refuse to the far side of the moon, and passed away soon after, leaving his son without inheritance nor means of livelihood.

But Im was a bright lad, and an ambitious one. He meant to go to the top. And looking up, one evening, he saw the top—the high tower room of Piras Tindeval. What did he have to lose? He would only starve if he remained without magic in a city of magic, and about Hirstel lay the empty sands of the desert, vast and reputably impassable.

What wards might lie above, what dangers? He and all of Hirstel knew the high chamber of the Prince-Sorcerer had its guardian. Yet Im began ascending, finding easy hand and footholds on the deeply carved shaft, decorated with the forms of the thousand and fourteen Demons of Droga. Now and again, Im found himself face to face with the horrifying visage of one of these, carved in the lustrous black marble, or was forced to place his hand on some repulsive element of their anatomy. Above blazed the bright stars of ever-clear skies. He could see the silvered dunes that surrounded the city walls from this vantage. What lay beyond?

Then he pulled himself stealthily through a narrow but unbarred window. There was no guard to be seen, nothing but a plain table of some dark, polished wood and, on that table, a silver chest. Carefully, quietly, he approached it and removed the book bound in red leather that he found within.

Im had but opened it when he felt a massive hand on his shoulder. "Hold," came a deep groan of a voice. The creature—a demon, obviously—stood a head taller than the tallest man he had ever seen, and was allover red, a deep wine-red. He turned to face it. What else was there to do?

Its naked body was smooth, featureless, with no obvious musculature nor reproductive organs. Where a man might have a face, was a flat, blank expanse of shining red. Somewhat like a well-polished shield, the boy thought. "I am Qu'orthseth." The words came as the wind-driven sand. "I regret that I must slay you, young man."

Im considered leaping from the window. Surely dashing his brains out on the cobblestones far below would be preferable to being dismembered by this demon. He had heard tales of bits and pieces of would-be thieves being scattered about the base of the tower.

"You couldn't look the other way and let me slip out, could you?" It didn't hurt to ask.

Qu'orthseth slowly shook its head. "I may not. The duty laid upon me is to destroy all those who enter this tower room of Piras Tindeval. To do otherwise is to break my oath."

"O, mighty Demon," said Im, "slay me if you must. First, though," he inquired, "will you answer my questions? If you do intend to take my life, then surely you are fulfilling your promise. You don't think I can escape you?"

"This is true. Of course I can kill you anytime so there is no hurry. I must admit, conversation is somewhat lacking in this room. The boss rarely comes up here and when he does, he doesn't have time to talk."

"How," wondered the youngster, "did he get you here in the first place?"

The monstrous form hung its head. Having no face, its expressions were limited. "He rescued me from prison," Qu'orthseth admitted, "and demon prison is a very bad place indeed. Far worse than being stuck in a lonely tower room for a couple centuries. As long as I fulfill my oath here, I can remain. The moment I might break it—" Fortunately, the demon had shoulders, so it added to its repertoire of expressions by shrugging. "Well, I'll be immediately whisked back to torment in my native hell."

"Ah. And your oath is to protect the book?" Im had hopes of finding a loophole.

"Not exactly. The wording in these contracts must be quite precise in laying out what is expected on each side. For himself, Piras promises to keep me free from my prison as long as I follow my own vow of slaying anyone—and the wording makes it clear that 'anyone' includes small animals—who enters this room. Other than the prince himself, naturally.

"I have had to knock off a few cats over the years," the great red creature admitted, with definite regret in its impossibly deep voice. "And I like cats. People, not so much."

Yes, yes, they were cat burglars. May we get back to the story?

Hmm, that idea wouldn't work, then. If only Qu'orthseth were tied to the book rather than the tower, he might have come up with a trick to earn his freedom. Im looked again to the window.

The demon caught his intention. "Don't think of leaping. I could catch you before you reached the ground and then I would take you apart, piece by piece, without further delay. With luck, I could make it last a while to relieve my boredom.

"But," it rumbled on, "conversing with you is preferable. Behave and I shall break your neck quickly, dismembering you later as a warning to others."

Im shrugged, in apparent resignation. "Would it hurt if I looked into the book?" he asked. "I might as well know what it is I am dying for."

"It is permitted," spoke the demon. "Be aware that no spells in the book of my master would work against me. I can not be destroyed nor turned from my duty, even by the most powerful magic of this world." But maybe of its own world, thought Im. That wouldn't do him any good. Unless he could call up a demon of greater power?

The grimoire still lay on the dark slab before him. Im leafed through it, not hurrying. He was relieved to see it was written in straight-forward Zikem, which he and everyone else in Hirstel could readily read. "Are there many powerful demons in your realm?" he asked of Qu'orthseth.

Was that low rhythmic sound, something alike to distant thunder over the desert, a chuckle? "Very many. Know that they may not harm me nor prevent my actions as long as I am bound here by my geas."

That made sense. Otherwise, the demon police would have come and swept it back to its cell. Or wherever they kept their prisoners. But demons could do other things. Hmm, there was named Sebuchax, the mighty archfiend who had built this tower for the Prince-Sorcerer. What could be built could be—

Destroyed! He put his mind around the proper spell, getting it well fixed, and then called out, "Sebuchax—"

Well, I won't give you the rest of the words for fear of blasting your souls. Then who would listen to my stories?

The words of the spell, of course, were only for focus; it is the mind that really does the work and Im had a mind that was up to the task. He tucked the thick book under his arm and waited as the walls began to crumble about him, Sebuchax—in the form of an immense ebony shadow—demolishing that which he had once created. If he were dashed to death as the edifice fell, so be it, but Im expected a different outcome. Surely enough, the great red demon caught him up and carried him to a nearby rooftop. Im was not quite certain how Qu'orthseth accomplished this, as it had no wings, but was willing to let that question wait.

"That was unexpected," rumbled his companion.

"The tower no longer stands, nor does the room you guarded exist. Your duty there is ended."

"But I am still obligated to destroy you, boy." As Im had assumed and expected.

"And what will happen when you do?"

This query Qu'orthseth pondered for a few moments. It then slowly answered, "I would be instantly whisked back to my own world and prison."

"Then you must keep me alive, mustn't you? It is your only way to remain in this world."

What was the creature thinking? wondered Im, as its blank visage regarded him for a rather long time. "I could blast your mind and store you away somewhere," it stated, at last, "leaving that grimoire behind." It looked at the book Im held. "My master would be less likely to seek me then. He cares only for the safety of his spell-book."

Im guessed at the reason for the demon's apparent reluctance. "And how long could you keep me alive?"

"Not long enough. That sort of thing can go wrong, too, and then I would be—elsewhere."

"Ah." Im held up the leather-bound volume, "With this, I could do much for both of us. And," he went on, "prolong my life greatly." Wasn't Piras reputedly close to a thousand years of age?

Qu'orthseth nodded. "The book means nothing to me. I was to guard the room, not what was in it." From their high perch, it looked out over the desert. "Does that sand go on forever?" it asked. "I know little of your world, in truth."

"There's only one way to find out," replied Im. "So let us put as much distance between ourselves and the prince as we can, as quickly as we can."

"Agreed," said the demon, grasping the young burglar and rising into the air. "Westward?" it asked.

"As good a direction as any," said Im.

This was written as a stand-alone short story but became the first chapter of the fantasy novel 'The Ways of Wizardry.'

The Walled Garden

I will not regret our love, nor my daring to climb the garden walls to taste of it.

She, my beloved, my Adina—from the time we were children playing tag in the shadows of marketplace awnings, we had known we were meant for each other. I would catch her in some secluded doorway and steal a kiss, promising someday to ask her father for her hand. As she grew into a rose of great beauty, I anticipated that day with all my soul.

Yet such a beauty will catch other eyes. So it was that Sultan Khalid's vizier came one day to her father's door and paid him a great price for his Adina—my Adina. I watched the curtained litter bear her away to Khalid's palace. It bore her away to be a jeweled ornament of his harem, a flower that grew only in his walled garden.

That walled garden was death to any whole man who dared enter. Yet enter I must. Was I never to see my Adina again, never to hold her, never to consummate the love that had burned within us both? On a moonless night, when the wind blew hot from the desert sands, I scaled those high walls and entered Khalid's forbidden garden, his garden of jasmine-scented delight.

Secreted behind the arbored roses, I awaited some sign of my lost love. Would Adina walk in this garden? Was she near me? Should I dare search for her?

Laughter drifted through my night. Two young, beautiful and most scandalously dressed—or undressed—women were walking along the green marble pathway near my hiding place. "She will come around," said the one, laughing. "Give her time. And give me a kiss."

The two embraced as lovers would, their hands exploring each others bodies. I had heard of such things but found it most astonishing. I also found my manhood responding in a most astonishing manner. Suddenly I heard a sharp intake of breath. It was my Adina, who had come upon the two entwined women.

"Come, join us," invited one. "It is better than with a man anytime."

The other smiled. "She has not yet been with a man, have you, little one?" Adina shook her head, hesitantly. She was clad nearly as scantily as they—at that moment I ached for her as I never had before.

"She pines still for he who loved her. He is dead to you, girl, and you to him. Best it be that way. Let us find some private pillowed place," she told her companion. "Leave the little one to her tears." The two slipped away into the perfumed darkness.

Adina fell upon an alabaster bench, weeping to the silence of her misfortune. I whispered her name from my hiding place. "Adina!"

"Who calls?" Her long black tresses fell back from her face as she peered questioningly about the garden. Her full bosom rose and fell beneath the diaphanous blouse that only partially covered her beauty. "Is there someone there to help me? Has Allah sent the aid for which I have prayed?"

"No, my Adina, He has brought your Hadi to you," I responded, stepping from my hidden bower.

"Hadi, my Hadi!" She flew into my arms. "The Sultan has not yet called for me. I—I am still pure for you, my Hadi."

"You must come with me, my love," I asserted, "and we shall flee together."

She pulled back. "No, my Hadi, it can not be. How could I scale these walls? Where could we go? I must remain here. But," she continued fiercely, "I will not allow Khalid to be the first to have me! Tonight, I give myself to my true love.

"My first love," she whispered, "my only love." Taking her hand, I led her to my hiding place behind the arbor.

Rose petals were our bed, that dark, still night. There I took her lips, full and red as the blossoms that overhung us; there I kissed each inch of her exquisite body before entering where no man had entered before. And there we slept the slumber of perfect peace, forgetful of our tomorrow.

Only to awaken with the splashing of the sun into our eyes. "You must be away, my love," Adina urged, as I gathered her in a final kiss. Alas, it was too late. The eunuchs were searching the garden for her and discovered us there, holding to each other in our farewell embrace.

Now, as I lay my neck upon the block, I look into Adina's sightless eyes, gaze upon the tangled black locks surrounding her head where it lies upon the tessellated floor, and know we soon shall embrace once again in Paradise.

The Pimp

I NEVER INTENDED to be a pimp. It was my sister who wondered *Who will protect me* and *How else will we survive?* So I did as she asked but could not protect her from all things. The consumption took Elaine one December morning when the sun barely limped into overcast skies. The priests refused burial to her worn husk and so she went to an unmarked pit outside the city walls. I have since donated moneys for a graveyard for such as she.

Others I protected since and I always treated them well, taking only my due. They were not 'mine,' as another man in my trade might claim; rather, I was theirs, their servant, their agent. As ever, some prospered and some wasted. That was not for me meddle in. I could protect them from many dangers but not from themselves.

Is it so far from helping women sell their bodies on the street to aiding those who would sell them on stage? There was Kate, one of those for whom I procured and protected, who first spoke to me of being an actress. She was no great talent and long forgotten, but I found her a role and took my usual cut. Oh, aye, she needed as much protection in the theaters as she did on the streets!

Broad-hipped Kate led to others and soon I was handling two groups of women though, indeed, more than a few passed back and forth from one to the other—or worked both careers at the once. That mattered not to me. But, increasingly, I found myself leaving the career of pimp for the semi-respectable one of theatrical agent.

I found lodging in the theater district and made one of my two small rooms an office. On the third floor it was, the least expensive choice, but I enjoyed the view, for I had made sure to take rooms that looked onto the street. It was a street of theaters, and crowded with light and bodies much of the night. So it was I slept days, mostly—no change there from my old life. There was a sign by the ground floor, directing one up the steep stairs, and another on my door. Merely my name, Mr. R. Bailey, and *Agent* beneath it.

In my way, I was still pimp, I knew. That had never bothered me before—not since I first chose that way of life—and bothered me not now.

So you find me today, owner of two theaters and of properties scattered through the city. Shabby tenements, many; yes, slum lord you might call me but I try to take care of the places. Never be it said I did not give a square deal. My offices now fill that entire building where first I rented and I myself have a good-enough house. Not a grand house, mind you, for what would be the point of that when I've none to share it with?

None save the ghost of Elaine, which has followed me from lodging to lodging. I see her homely, heavy-jawed face, the big head perched on the twig-thin body, as pale as the day she died. Oh, lovers have come and gone but how could I have any of them stay when she hovered close? I hear her cough in the night and wonder that others do not. Elaine, hacking up the ruin of her lungs—I remember the blood on her lips each morn. I look for it when I glimpse my sister's specter but see none. Perhaps there is none left.

Does she resent my success? It was Elaine who set me on the path, chose to name us *whore* and *pimp*, and then fell by the roadside. There is no blame due either of us. I have done what I thought best, what I could, what I must. But regrets crowd 'round when I sense her spirit with me, continuing our journey, even though her body gave up. I am not old; I could yet find a wife, have children, build that grand house I do not need. What point, otherwise?

I should not be wandering this house in the hours before dawn, alone. Alone with my possessions, the art that covers my walls, the fine porcelain in its cabinets, the silken robe wrapped about me. All this should be shared. Ah, Elaine, would that I could have shared it with you.

A deep hacking echœs through the empty rooms. I hear that much, lately. It seems it is with me always. I look to my embroidered linen kerchief and note how much blood I have coughed up this time.

The Biggest Mermaid

"ANOTHER SAILOR MISTOOK me for a manatee today," Muriel pouted. "I really must go on a diet."

"But my dear," protested her mother, "the blubber helps protect you from the cold of the depths, as with all sea creatures."

"Not much good if I can't entice a man or two to join me in those depths."

The older mermaid sighed. "Humans just don't appreciate a full figure these days."

"And there aren't near enough shipwrecks anymore," said a sister. "We could always depend on a drowning sailor every now and then."

Another sibling giggled. "They don't care that much about our figures!"

The family sat in an alcove amid the pink and white towers of a great coral reef, surrounded by treasure they had found and gathered. They knew nothing of its value, nor did they care, but they liked the pretty baubles, the flashing red and green stones, the shiny gold coins and jewelry. Now and again a mermaid would rub off the algæ and coral that had begun to grow on them. This was usually because they were bored, and soon they would find some other undersea pleasure to take their interest.

"All we see anymore is those who have already drowned and washed out to us." The drowned men could be animated for a while, with a bit of magic, but that wasn't really the same. And then the fishes tended to nibble at them too.

"Too cold," stated Muriel. "Too bloodless."

Heads nodded in agreement, heads of dark luxuriant locks, floating and writhing in the eddies rising through the spreading branches of the coral. A parrot fish glided by. One of the maids reached out and snatched it, biting into the brightly-colored swimmer with strong sharp teeth. "Not bloodless here," she spoke between dainty nibbles, "but cold." The others sighed.

This was no good, thought Muriel. "I'm going to go find a warm-blooded man," she proclaimed. "No, a hot-blooded man! And I'm not coming back till I do."

She searched along many coasts without much luck. Once she even pulled herself up on the shore and posed enticingly. Someone called, "Another whale has beached itself! We need to push it back into the water!" Muriel did not wait for them to make the attempt. Then, as she swam along the shores of Rum Cay, sometimes close to the sunny, sandy beaches, sometimes diving into the dark depths, the mermaid spied a little harbor and, in that harbor, a little dock. On it sat an old man, dozing, a fishing rod in his hands. She swam up and tugged on his line to awaken him.

The old fisherman rubbed his eyes when she surfaced and gave him her sauciest smile.

"I'll be! A mermaid." He looked her up and down—as much of her as he could see. "I've sailed far more than seven seas in me life, gal, but I believes ye are the biggest I've iver laid eyes on."

Muriel scowled at the rude old fellow and was ready to flip over and dive back into the depths. "Don't bother me none," he continued. "Some might say thar be more of ye to love."

The man was old and bent and had a long white beard. But he was a man. The mermaid smiled at him again, taking care not to show too many teeth. "Why don't you jump in and show me?"

"Not me, gal. I know ye ladies of the sea has a way of drownin' yer lovers. Whether ye means to or not, I've niver been sartain."

Muriel had never drowned a man before she intended to. She took some pride in this. "What if I promise not to?" she asked.

"Will ye swear by Neptune, gal? A real oath?"

The mermaid hesitated. Oh, why not? "By Neptune I swear not to drown you, elderly mortal. Aye, and by Thalassa as well."

"Good enough. Those are powerful vows and I knows you'll

keep 'em." With that he threw off the ragged pair of shorts that were his only garment and jumped into the water.

"I always had me a hankering to find out what it's like to be with a mermaid. I seen a school of ye frolicking off the Cape of Good Hope once and almost dived in."

"You would have been drowned," she told him.

"So I reckoned! Best I waited till ye showed up, eh?"

"Quit talking, old fool, and come to me."

He was eager enough to do so at once. Ah, yes! The old salt was still virile. And she was careful to keep his head above water. Most of the time—passions did lead to occasional lapses of attention.

When both were fully sated, the old man rested, cradled in her ample arms, against her ample breasts and ample body. "Why do ye seek out mortals like me?" he asked, when his breath returned. He did need to cough up a little salt water. "Ain't you got no mermen?"

"They're stupid and ugly, and dangerous brutes. They mostly end up killing each other, so we seek mortal men. You're much nicer."

"Glad to hear it. Go again?" He leered in a somewhat repulsive manner.

"I think not." She had promised only not to drown the man. Nothing else. And she had been dieting long enough! Muriel sank her sharp teeth into his throat. The beard was no impediment.

And though he was a bit leathery he was full of hot blood.

The Passions of Penelope

...WE JOIN OUR heroine in Chapter 8:

"Avast there, wench!"

The pirate captain strode purposefully across the deck, stepping over the first mate's body, to roughly take Penelope into his muscular, tattooed arms.

"Yer me woman, now," he growled, his dark eyes glowing with a lust born in the fires of hell. "I've won ye fair 'n' square!"

"Oh, Captain Bard!" begged the young beauty, "don't... stop..."

"Arrgh!" the buccaneer replied, pressing her against his main mast.

"Pieces of eight!" added his parrot.

"Jest let me at this bodice!" His powerful hands grasped at the cloth covering her full, heaving bosom. "What the divil!" he exclaimed in sudden surprise, pulling out his cutlass as the Indian chief leaped down from the poop deck.

"Penelope my woman!" claimed the chiseled savage. "She belong on top my totem pole!"

"We'll see about that, me hearty!" The two, driven by their insatiable craving for Penelope's perfect body, circled with sword and tomahawk in hand.

"Gentlemen!" Her sea-green eyes flashing, full rosy lips parted, the object of their quarrel stepped between them. "I'm woman enough for the two of you!" she announced, passionately ripping open her bodice to expose full, creamy breasts.

The desire-drunk combatants gaped at her with amazement, then lowered their weapons, looking each other's hard, sweating bodies over thoughtfully.

"Me like threesome!" decided the bronze warrior. "You heap good looking sailor!"

"Yer not so bad yerself, matey! Let's head fer me cabin!"

Chapter 9: Beauregard returns from the war!

The Horns of Fœrie

HE SHOULDN'T BE able to hear the traffic from here. Arthur's office was a windowless room on the fifth floor, well insulated from the tumult of the city that lay all about the building. Yet he had distinctly heard a horn. He was sure of it.

Arthur went to the door and looked down the hall, both directions. Nothing to be seen. Shaking his head, he returned to his desk and his numbers.

That evening, on the bus, he thought he heard an unfamiliar note arise amid the customary, unnoticed din, the background of an hundred, a thousand, such bus rides. It seemed to come from somewhere other than the busy streets, somewhere far away. Soft, distant, haunting, it echœd a moment and faded. He looked about at his fellow riders. None seemed to have noticed anything unusual.

Nor did he that evening. Arthur slept solidly and had quite forgotten about it the next day.

But night came again, as ever it dœs. Falling into sleep, once more he heard the horn. Closer now, it seemed, yet still somehow immeasurably far distant. He sat up to see a faint glimmer, a mist of moonlight between dark, thick columns. The trunks of great forest trees, he realized, as it faded, returning him to the darkness of his bedroom, broken only by the glow of the hands on his alarm clock. A dream, Arthur told himself, and fell slowly, fitfully, back into sleep.

A dream that persisted and haunted; a dream that called to him, for Arthur Reed yearned for more than his gray daily life, the dreary office, the empty apartment. He had known such dreams before, when he was a boy, and forgotten them. Forever, he had thought.

Now the memories wafted back, as fitful breezes do that toss the dark scented pines of some lost valley, as a longing for something long lost that he could not quite name. He saw the way more clearly each time the horn sounded, sounded more and more strong, more and more near. At last he took a step toward those woods that seemed a world away, to see them again fade. But had he spied shapes moving among the trees, men and horses? Had he heard fair voices crying?

Each day he harked to that horn. It blew more often and the world where he lived and worked became less real to him. He seemed to spend hours looking at his papers and accomplishing nothing.

"Something must be done about Reed," said his employer. "He was always a good man. A solid man." He shook his head. Yes, something must be done. He'd give him a little more time but then—perhaps he would have to let him go.

It had done no good to speak to him. The man had barely been listening, he thought, as if other more important concerns occupied his mind.

And Arthur's eyes had seen past him, seen moss-covered hoary oaks rising in a forest man did not know. He had gone deeper into those woods each time the horn had called. He stood now in the shadows, listening to the riders, somewhere near, crying out to one another, the great tall horses neighing in the exhilaration of their headlong rush through the wild.

"The hunt is on!" came a voice near at hand. Arthur turned to see who spoke and knew this was no man such as dwelt in the world to which he was born. All in green he was, upon a stamping mist-gray steed, and the light in his eyes spoke of ages unknown.

"The hunt?"

"The Wild Hunt, lad," came the reply. With a laugh, the huntsman urged his horse forward, crying back over his shoulder, "We follow the stag. Run with us, if ye will!"

The forest faded, as before, leaving Arthur in his gray window- less office. *I can not stay here,* he told himself. *The horns of fœrie have called and I must go.* Had he not sought them all his life? Out into the street he went, moving as a sleepwalker.

"The hunt," he murmured. "I must find the hunt." People moved away from him as he stumbled forward. Their faces began to blur, to be replaced by other visions. The forest again rose about him. The Hunt was somewhere off that direction. He could hear the wild riders.

Come! Come! called their voices. *Come join the hunt!*

"I will!" cried Arthur, rushing forward, free at last. "I will! I come!"

As he ran, he fell to all-fours. He saw his hands become great cloven hooves. He felt the heavy antlers that spread wide from his head. Behind him, rose the horns of the hunt.

He who was once Arthur Reed fled into the forest.

Marian

YES, I KNEW Robin. A Robin, neither the first nor the last to name himself so. For a century and more, from Nottingham to Lincoln to York, they plied the robber's trade. Some cast a longer shadow than others.

Some, they say, were gentlemen. Some claimed to be the confidantes of kings, be it Richard or Edward. Some were base in birth; some were base in spirit.

But my Robin? Ah, he was a gallant fellow, though a yeoman born. He knew the tales of chivalry and, mayhap, he took them over seriously. Why else might he choose to woo a young noblewoman? Many a night I could readily have laughed at his pretenses, his phrases more suited to the tongue of a minstrel than that of a fighting man—much less a bandit.

Indeed, they might have been invented for him by a minstrel. I remember a disreputable jongleur with whom he used to drink. Alan was he styled. Long has it been since I heard his ale-soaked songs. But that matters not; it was from Robin's lips those words of love fell, and I knew they told what was in his heart, whatever their origin. Young women like to hear such words.

Some long to hear them. Not I. They were but a way to relieve the tedium of my life. Would that I could have been as Robin, roaming free in the woods! That was my heart's desire, not to listen to his pretty pronouncements.

Of a summer's night, when daylight lingered into the dusk, I would steal away from my father's house and make tryst with my Robin. In the garb of my maid I would go. Yes, as a common serving girl I went and sat with him and his merry ruffians and the tavern-gœrs, and they would laugh and call me Maid Marian, and there was not one 'my lady' to be heard.

Save from Robin, ever courteous when we walked beneath the stars and the great oaks of his forest hideaways. Not so courteous in his love-making, though!

They hanged them all there one day, Robin and his men, from

one of those great oaks. That among them was the infamous Robin, the sheriff's men knew not nor did they most likely care. I knew.

Sir Guy told me of it when he rode home, home to me and my child with Robin's eyes. He is a good man, my husband, good enough, and I can not fault him for doing his duty. Nay, not even if he held the rope in his own hands. Robin had become no more than a dream to me by then, fading before the dawn of new days.

Alan, I understand, made up a different ending for our story.

afterword

I CONFESS THAT I never considered myself a writer of the short story. That is now up to my readers to decide. There had been but a scattered few stories over the years while most of my attention was turned to the novel and to pœtry. What stories I did write had a tendency to grow into novels.

Recently, I found myself writing more stories—enough to fill a small collection. Those found here all tend toward the fantastic; some day a 'mainstream' book of short stories might appear, or even more fantasies.

Aside from 'The Book, the Beast, and the Burglar,' these stories have no relationship to my fantasy novels. They are not set in the same worlds. I may never revisit some of the worlds found in these pages. You, however, are invited to visit them as often as you might wish.

Stephen Brooke 2021

www.ingramcontent.com/pod-product-compliance
Lightning Source LLC
Chambersburg PA
CBHW030147200626
46812CB00015B/1743